I0760457

FALL OF THE HARVEST MOON

NEW WORLD SHIFTERS BOOK FOUR

NINA WALKER

KIMBERLY LOTH

Cover designed by MiblArt

Edited by Ailene Kubricky

and Cookie Lynn

PROLOGUE
ABI

PEOPLE HAVE BEEN TAKING choices away from me for as long as I can remember. I was raised by a community that treated me as less than everyone else. I was Abigail, the unimportant claimed girl everyone would soon forget. Not Abi, the girl who had ambitions for herself. When I came to the wolf city, I had foolish hopes that things would change for the better, but they only changed for the worse. Despite the lessons in pack hierarchy, I had no real idea what was in store for me, and when I learned what I had to do, I didn't sleep for three days.

How could I be expected to fight for a beta when I hated them? To become the wife of somebody I didn't love? To raise children with a man who would most likely frequent brothels, only to set me aside once I aged beyond fertility? Not that it mattered—none of those men liked me any more than I liked them. I was never going to get engaged. That was a fate left to the prettier and more flirtatious girls. Flirting has never been my strength. Even now, when I know it might get me kinder men, I still can't figure it out.

I'm actually lucky to still be alive, considering what I've done. But maybe it would've been better to die instead of rotting in the mating house. Cutting through Joanna's and Grady's ropes had been more than just an act of setting them free; it had been an act of defiance. My personal rebellion. I took back my power in that moment. Finally making a choice worth living for.

That's the memory I cling to every time I think I can't possibly endure another day in this mating house. I stare at the ceiling above my bed. There's a water stain that looks like a bunny rabbit. We raised rabbits back home. I was never allowed to get attached to them because they were food, but I still liked cuddling them.

"Earth to Abi." Jasmine snaps her fingers in front of my face, and I startle. "Are you alive in there?"

I blink and refocus on the task at hand, preparing myself for the day ahead. I need to get up and get going. The older women make the wolf city run, but we mating-house girls make the wolf city grow. I sit up and stretch, reaching for the dress I had laid out earlier when I had come to bed. It's short and form-fitting, easy to get on and off.

"Sorry," I mutter. "Can you pass me the lipstick?"

Jasmine rummages around in a makeup bag and retrieves the lightest color. She knows I hate the dark stuff. Of the twenty girls who live in our mating house, she's my closest friend here. She's funny, kind, and optimistic. And she's also so deep in denial about what's going on here that her mind isn't always with us. Some of the others make fun of her for it, but it makes me want to protect her. She's been in the house longer than anyone else and is getting close to retirement. The worst part is the way she talks about her children as if she'll see them once she leaves this house. She must know it's not true, but still, she pretends.

"Do you think Henry and Luke are together? I had them in the same year. Irish twins. I bet they're together. They're probably reading by now. Do you think they know they're brothers?"

I swallow hard and then smile at her. "I'm sure they do."

It's a lie. I'm certain that they're being raised like all the other wolf shifter boys, grouped by age until they're old enough to be ranked and given assignments. On the rare occasion that a girl is born, she's whisked away to Chicago to be raised with the other lunas, never to be seen again. The only exceptions are the children the betas have with their wives. Motherhood isn't something we mating-house girls will ever get to experience, no matter how many Henrys and Lukes we have. Those are the sixth and seventh names I've heard her talk about. I wonder how many kids she's had in total, or if she even knows.

Jasmine hums wistfully to herself and leans toward

the mirror, applying a swipe of mascara across her already dark lashes. It makes her brown eyes impossibly beautiful. Why didn't she get picked for a beta's wife? She's so pretty, so kind and sweet. She pats her belly gently. "I think I might be pregnant again." Her voice is filled with excitement. "I love being pregnant."

Her pronouncement makes my own stomach twist. I knew what I was getting myself into, and still, this is worse than I could've imagined. And the rumor is that our house isn't even the worst one. Here, the men are punished for being violent toward us, though we still go to bed with bruises some nights, and there are limits to how many men can frequent our beds each day. Some of the other houses have no rules or limits. It's wrong. It's all so wrong.

"I hope I never get pregnant," I say with conviction. What I don't say is that giving up children against my will to be raised by other people would be worse than giving up my body to these men who care nothing for me. To give the pack a child would be to give them what they want, like some kind of sick reward for what they're doing here. I know that having a child means I'd be able to leave the mating house for the duration of the pregnancy, but still. I don't want to have a child just to give it up.

"Oh, but pregnancy is the best," Jasmine argues. "You get to live in the fancy house, and they treat you like a queen for the entire nine months, plus a month after while you're healing from delivery."

I scoff. "And isn't delivery terrible? Some women die."

She shrugs as if death wouldn't be the worst thing, but given the circumstances, maybe it wouldn't be. She finishes with her makeup and helps me with my hair, and we go down to the parlor room where we're to meet our "dates" for the evening.

"Abigail..." Madame Lindy, our housemistress, stops me at the stairs with a cross expression. She's never been very kind to me, and I wonder what I did wrong now. Yesterday, she scolded me for trying to get out of my date. But it's not my fault that I ate something bad and puked all day. Thankfully, my date was quick, and I didn't throw up on him. Though, that would've been amusing. "You're a week late. Why didn't you say something?" She raises a notebook as if to hit me with it.

"Late to what?" My stomach twists again, and I wonder what it is I've been eating.

Jasmine claps her hands, and Madame Lindy shushes her. Jasmine quiets and fusses with her dress.

"Your period is late, Abi. You were due to start seven days ago."

Her words ring in my ears. They don't make sense. I'm not late. I can't be late. But then again, I haven't been keeping track—I didn't want to face the reality of a late menstrual cycle. My whole body goes rigid, and my knees weaken. *I'm late . . .*

"Back upstairs." She points. "No dates for you until we can confirm that you're not pregnant."

"And if you are, you know what that means," Jasmine practically cheers.

"A baby," I say, my voice flat and emotionless, not at all reflecting the torment I feel inside. I can't be pregnant. I just can't be. I've only been here for three months, and that seems too fast for it to have already happened.

"It means the good life!" Jasmine giggles manically, turning on our mistress. "I think I'm pregnant too, Madame Lindy. Should I go upstairs with Abi?"

"No," our mistress barks back. "You're not due to bleed for another two weeks."

Jasmine grabs her breasts and flops her head to the side dreamily. "But I can tell. My boobs always hurt when I'm pregnant, and they've been hurting all day today."

Madame Lindy rolls her eyes. "Back to work with you, Jasmine. We can't keep your date waiting."

My mind races as I climb back up the stairs. Pregnant. I remember when my older brother's wife got pregnant. She was so excited. But then, three months later, she wasn't pregnant anymore. Maybe that's what'll happen to me. My body will reject the baby, and I'll never have to hand him over. I barely make it back to my room when Madame Lindy pokes her head in.

She tosses me a stick. "Here, you need to pee on this."

"What is it?"

"A test to tell whether you're pregnant or not."

She follows me into the bathroom.

"Are you going to watch me?" I ask, mortified.

"Yes. Too many girls have learned how to fake the results. I have to watch you all now."

I don't look at her while I take care of things. It's too embarrassing. Though, after all the things I've done with men, I shouldn't be embarrassed to have my body on display for anyone anymore.

I hand her back the stick, and she sets it on the counter.

"Now what?" I ask.

"Now we wait. If two lines appear, you go pack your stuff. If just one, then I'll make some calls and get another man down here for you tonight."

I should want those two blue lines, but I don't. I'd rather she make the call.

After what seems like ages, she picks up the stick and shows it to me. "Congratulations. You're growing the pack. Go get your stuff."

I put my hand on my stomach.

I'm growing a monster.

CHAPTER 1

IT'S BEEN three days since Ryne was bitten, and I haven't left his side. I know there is so much going on outside, so much I should be worrying about with the Resistance and the lycans and wolf-pack hierarchy, but I can't leave my mate. I have to wait with him. I've banished both Justin and Nico from the tent. They keep telling me it would be more merciful to kill Ryne, but I can't let them do it. He's still alive, and they thought he'd be dead by now.

Callum keeps giving him herbs for the pain, but I don't think it's doing much. His body writhes most of the time. Occasionally, he comes to, looking me in the eye and telling me that he loves me. And then I lose him again.

It's the middle of the night, and I'm lying next to him, my head on his sweaty shoulder.

"Poppy." Ryne's voice cuts through the darkness

even though it's soft. I jerk up and look him in the eyes, to search them for a sign that he's getting better. They're brighter than they were last night, but he's very pale.

"It's okay. You can go back to sleep."

He shakes his head. "I don't think I'll be alive much longer. I can feel myself slipping away. Poppy, I love you. Promise me you'll take care of yourself."

I lean over him. "Don't talk like that."

His hand grips my waist. "I mean it. You need to fight for your freedom." He's more coherent than I've seen him since I bit him. That has to be the sign I need, right?

I shake my head. "You're not dying."

"Yes, I am. No one survives the bite. Even me. You need to let me go."

Tears fall onto his chest. "Not yet." I know I'm going to lose him, but I'm not ready. Not by a long shot.

He pulls me closer. I'm surprised he has the strength. He places a hand on the back of my head and presses his lips against mine. For a moment, I forget that he's dying. Forget that he's writhing in pain. Forget that I may never kiss him again. Our lips and tongues move furiously against one another. The desperate last kiss of a dying man.

And then he falls limp in my arms.

A sob bursts from my lungs. This is it. This is the end. His breathing stops, and his body goes impossibly still, as if it's not a body anymore, as if he's not Ryne anymore.

"No, no, no," I cry out, shaking him. "Don't go. Don't leave me."

But it's useless . . . Ryne is dead.

I don't want to believe it. I can't possibly accept it. But deep down, I know it's true, and no amount of crying or pleading is going to bring him back. After all the death and trauma I've had to endure, this one will break me. I will never be the same. I cling to his body, knowing it will soon grow cold, but this is a luxury I never had with my sister. I can hold him for as long as I want.

I should go get Callum and the others. We're going to need to prepare the body for burial. Or will they want to burn it? The thought of his beautiful body being engulfed in flames makes my stomach pinch, and I lie down again, returning my head to his shoulder, and whisper confessions of love and regret into his ear. I never want to leave him—this beautiful man who I killed.

And so I don't.

Sometime later, when the birds begin to greet the dawn, I get up the nerve to face reality. I'm unable to look at Ryne's face as I hurry from the tent. I have to find Ryne's packmates to let them know what's happened. They were right about him dying, so they won't be surprised, but I need to get this over with before they find him in there.

"Poppy, are you okay?" Justin asks, standing up near

the long-dead campfire. I briefly wonder when it went out. Did it die around the same time Ryne did?

A labored inhalation later and Nico is at my side, catching me as my knees buckle. Hoarse sobs rip from my body as the grief hits me all at once. "He's dead," I gasp. "Ryne's dead."

Nico steadies me and then looks me right in the eye, his voice careful. "Are you sure?"

I don't know why, but that asinine question sends rage through my core. "Am I sure?" I bite out, pushing him off me. "Am I sure? I don't know, Nico. Ryne took his last breath in my arms last night, but maybe I was mistaken." My voice doesn't sound like me. This is some other Poppy, the Poppy who has been ruined by death. First, I lost Willow, and I only survived it because I found Joanna and Ryne. And now she's left me for our enemies, and Ryne is gone forever. This angry Poppy, this rageful Poppy, *she's* the new me, and *this* is my life now.

"Poppy." Justin inches forward, his eyes flashing to the tent and then back to me. "We'd have felt his death through the pack bond. But we felt nothing."

I stare at them, wondering how they could be so cruel.

"According to our bond, he's not dead yet," Nico insists.

Time seems to still, hanging like a question mark in midair. I know what happened.

Together, they sprint past me and into the tent. I

follow them in, barely registering that Callum and Faye are awake and in the tent now too. It seems everyone has to see for themselves that Ryne is really dead; they can't take my word for it.

"I don't know what's going on with the pack bond, but I know what happened last night." Tears pour down my face, sadness lapping over the anger. Ryne left me. He stopped breathing. He stopped moving. His body grew cold. *He's gone.*

I can't even bear to look at him anymore, knowing that his soul is no longer there. But I have to. I have to prove to the others that I'm not crazy.

"Here, let me." Callum kneels next to Ryne and presses his fingers to Ryne's neck. It's the first time I've let myself look at Ryne's face in death. He looks the same but different. Right but wrong. Here but not.

Another sob wracks me.

"I'm so sorry, Poppy," Faye whispers, standing at my side in the entrance to the tent. It's perhaps the first kind thing she's ever said to me, but it does nothing to make me feel better. Nothing ever could or ever will. Not without Ryne. She grips my hand, but I shake her off.

"He's got a pulse," Callum says, disbelieving.

"But he's obviously not breathing," I state woodenly, pointing to his chest. "How can there be a pulse?"

"I don't know. None of this makes sense." Callum looks up at me and shakes his head. "But since when did wolf shifters or lycanthropes make sense?"

Could he really be alive? I drop to my knees on

Ryne's other side, pushing Justin out of my way, and briefly press my lips to Ryne's. They're cold. Too cold. Cruelly cold. "What's happening here? Are you dead or not?" I whisper to him, wondering if perhaps he can hear me. He doesn't look like himself. He has to be dead. Pulse or no pulse.

"Our bond indicates he's not dead," Justin insists. "Trust me, we'd know if our alpha was gone."

Hope burns through my every cell, and I pray it's not false hope because I don't think I could handle this being some cruel twist of fate. "But he's so cold . . ."

"I don't understand," Faye interrupts, hands on her hips and glowering down at all of us. "He was burning up, but now he's cold? He was dead, but just kidding, he's alive? Which is it?"

There she is. I glare daggers at her, and she holds her hands up. "Hey, don't shoot the messenger. I'm just stating the obvious here." She's right. I know she is, but I don't have to like it.

"Let's look at the facts." Callum goes into doctor-scientist mode, pacing the tent. "Ryne was bitten by a lycan, and no wolf shifter has ever survived a lycan bite before."

"Fact," Justin and Nico say in unison.

"But, the difference here is that Poppy was the one to bite him, and she's kissed him several times since, even though it's close to the full moon, and she shouldn't have."

Blood drains from my face. I can't believe I didn't

remember not to do that. We'd been so careful not to kiss near the full moon since my lycan saliva sedates him, but I was so distracted and desperate over these last three days that I forgot. "What are you saying?"

"You're not just anyone to Ryne." A ring of excitement lightens Callum's voice, and he bounces on the balls of his feet. "You're his fated mate."

"Which means?" I'm not following his line of thinking.

"Which means, if my theory is correct, that your bite and your saliva, however painful and dangerous they may be, won't actually kill him."

"And why on earth not?" Faye asks incredulously, and I squeeze Ryne's hand, hoping that Callum could somehow be right. His heart is still beating, so he's still here when he shouldn't be.

"We can't intentionally kill our fated mates. It's one of the things we're taught as pups," Nico says bluntly to Faye and then looks at me. "I thought you could accidentally kill him, but perhaps fate won't allow that either."

Callum agrees. "And maybe because it was you and not someone else who bit him . . ."

I finish his thought. "Ryne might be the first wolf shifter to survive the lycan virus."

And in that moment, that glorious death-defying moment, Ryne's eyes fly open.

CHAPTER 2

RYNE LEAPS OFF THE COT, eyes blazing and fists clenched. "Where's my father?" he growls.

No one utters a word. The others move away from him, but I step closer. He flicks his gaze around the tent.

"Wait, where am I?"

I reach for his hand, but he jerks it away. My heart stills, but I recognize he's disoriented. I take another step closer to him but don't try to touch him. "You're in the wilds. The medical tent. Remember, we brought you here after . . . after you got hurt." I don't want to alarm him with too much information even though we've been through so much over the last few months, especially during the last festival.

He frowns. "The last thing I remember was fighting with my father. He didn't kill me?"

I blink back tears as I recall that awful moment. "No. He didn't."

"So what happened?"

All of his muscles are taut, and a vein in his neck twitches. He's ready to attack. "You . . . you got hurt. We brought you out here."

He finally meets my eye. "And my father?"

"Dead."

"How long was I out?"

"A few days." I can't believe he's forgotten it all. He was awake and lucid for some of it. We talked, he begged me to let him go, and he told me he loved me, that it wasn't my fault. But all that seems to have been erased from his mind in the last few hours.

He nods and finally relaxes. He sinks down onto the cot, and I risk sitting next to him. He doesn't move away from me, so I reach for his hand again, and he threads his fingers through mine. I lean my head on his shoulder.

"Tell me everything," he says, looking at Justin. "Did the Resistance fail? What happened to the other lycans?"

"They have abandoned the Resistance." Justin winces. "In fact, they're infecting humans on purpose now."

Ryne looks around the tent. "Where's Grady?"

My heart sinks at that question, for myself, for Joanna, for Ryne . . . for all of us.

Justin leans back on his heels. "He went with Laik. He thinks he'll have a better chance of keeping Joanna alive if he sides with them. Knox and Charlotte went too."

Ryne's face is horror-struck, and nobody moves a muscle for a long, tense moment until Callum crouches in front of us.

"How do you feel?" Callum asks, his voice smooth and gentle.

"It doesn't matter. I need to know what's going on. We should go to Chicago."

"Delphine and Elle are already there," Nico assures him. "Hopefully, Izaak is already the alpha."

"That's right. I forgot about the plan to put Elle's father on the throne. Everything is fuzzy. Why are we here instead of at my house?"

Justin sighs. "We thought this was safer. We didn't think you were going to make it."

"Why the hell not?" Ryne growls. "What happened to me?"

I hold my breath, and my stomach goes hard.

Callum's eyes sparkle as he examines Ryne. "You were bitten by a lycan." I wonder why he intentionally left my name out of it, but I can't help but be a little relieved, even if it's temporary.

Ryne leaps up. "And you didn't kill me right away?"

Justin shrugs. "We wanted to. Poppy wouldn't let us."

He glares down at me. "You would have me suffer?"

"I couldn't let you go." I stand to meet him, praying he'll understand. "And look. You're alive."

He jams a hand through his tangled hair. "How?"

Nico chuckles. "Well, you can't kill your fated mate. Remember?"

"What does that have to do with . . ." His voice fades away, and he turns to me, his jaw clenched. "*You* bit me?"

My face goes hot. "I didn't mean to. Your dad was going to kill you. I thought it was him that I was biting, not you."

"That was stupid and reckless. You could've gotten killed."

It's my turn to be angry now. I saved his life, and he's acting like I did something wrong. Which I guess I did, but still.

"You're alive, aren't you? If I hadn't intervened, you'd be dead."

"You should've killed me." Anger laces his voice.

How could he say something like that to me? "It was an accident." I reach for him, but he backs away as if I'm going to bite him all over again.

"How did my father die?" He looks at Justin, but I answer the question.

"I beheaded him," I confess. He's not going to get away with ignoring me. I get that he's angry that I bit him, but I didn't do it on purpose. And does he really think I would've allowed the others to kill him? He seems even angrier that I didn't, but I won't apologize for keeping my own mate alive. He did the same thing when I was the one who'd been bitten.

Ryne taps his teeth, and I can see the wheels in his head turning. "Who all knows it was you?"

"The other lycan that were on the mission and the people in this tent. Nobody else would've known it was me."

He nods once. "Good. I'm glad he's dead. It's time for me to go back to my pack. Things will be tense now without a king, and we don't need Anders doing anything stupid. Justin, Nico, let's go."

"Wait," Callum and I say at the same time.

"What?" Ryne asks.

Callum speaks before I do. "We have no idea what the lycan virus has done to your body."

"You're right. You can come with us. You're a competent doctor, and I trust you to keep me on track. We'll cut your hair to look like a claimed boy, and nobody else can know you're a lycan. But you will have to agree to be locked up during the full moons."

Callum looks pained at the idea, but he agrees anyway.

"What about me?" I ask. Ryne hasn't looked at me since he found out I bit him.

"You stay here. I don't ever want to see you again."

And with that, he leaves the tent.

Shock burns through me, a fire that is doused by shame. I can feel the pitying stares of everyone in the tent, and I refuse to meet their gazes. I don't know if I've ever been as angry with Ryne as I am right now. I jump up and storm after him, fists clenching and stomach a hollow pit. I might say something I'll regret, but at this point, who the hell cares? I've got nothing else to lose.

"You don't get to treat me like this," I yell at his back. "I saved your life!"

He ignores me, stalking off into the forest. He's already got his shirt off and is unbuttoning his pants when I catch up to him.

"Going to shift into your wolf and run away, huh?" I push his hard chest, but it's like pushing a tall unmovable wall. "I never knew you to be a coward, but I guess I should've known, considering how you never stood up to your father."

The second the words are out, I know I shouldn't have said them. He turns on me, knotted hair hanging to his shoulders and stormy blue eyes filled with malice. "I tried to kill my father according to the plan, but why should I have bothered when you did it for me?"

"So things didn't go according to your precious plan, and now you're going to take it out on me?" I throw my hands in the air. "I get that it would've been better for the pack hierarchy if you'd been the one to kill him, but, Ryne, you were losing the brawl. You needed my help." My voice softens at those last words, and I remember how scared I was that I was going to lose him.

He scoffs at that. "I was fine."

I meet his eyes. His breaths are short and fast, and his fists are clenched. I'm not used to seeing so much anger on him. I'm not scared of him, but I'm scared for him and for us. "Are you really so prideful that you'd have rather died and let him continue on as alpha king?"

His face becomes as unreadable as a mask. It would be easier if I could read him, if there was fury in his eyes or sadness in the turn of his lips, but there's nothing. His next words come out slowly, as if he wants me to consider them carefully. "I'm glad you're not dead, Poppy, and I'm angry that you could've died, but most of all, it hurts to look at you knowing how you betrayed me—how you *bit* me."

So this is about the bite? Is he serious right now? "The bite was an accident, but if I had to choose between biting you and you surviving the suffering it caused,"—I motion to his clearly intact and healed body —"or watching you die at the hands of your own father, then I would choose to see you alive." My voice cracks. "I love you, Ryne. You're my mate."

He winces and steps back. "And what *my mate* did to me is worse than death."

"How can you say that?" Tears blur my vision. My anger is all used up now. All I feel is desperation. If he leaves me, I don't think I can go on. I already lost him once. I was certain he was dead, and to have him back only to lose him by his own choice would break me.

"Because you should've let my betas kill me. Because I can feel the moon even now," he growls, his voice low and panicked. "It's already got a hold of me, and if I turn into a lycan next month, I'll lose my pack. There's no way they won't sense my new form if that happens."

And that's worse than dying? I don't understand how he could be upset by this. "Do you know what I went through last night? I was sure you were dead, and it destroyed me." My voice cracks, and I steady myself, peering up into his storm-cloud eyes. "So I get that you're afraid of what will happen if you become some kind of lycan, but I'll never regret that you're still alive."

His jaw clenches, and he leans closer. We're only inches apart now, so close I could touch him, kiss him, but I don't know that he'll ever let me do that again. "If I lose my pack, I'd rather be dead."

Those words rip my heart in two. "And what about me? No matter what you are, I love you. You wouldn't want to live for me? The woman who loves you?"

"You'd have me lose my pack to be with you?" His eyes travel up and down my face, searching for something that must be lacking, but I'm not sure what else he wants from me. "You call that love?"

"It's not like that."

He shakes his head and steps away, the space between us feeling like a million miles already. "Well, I don't give a damn about fate anymore. Fate may make it so I can't kill you, but it can't stop me from rejecting you."

The tears are pouring down my cheeks at this point, and I double over, heartbreak wracking through my body and searing deep down into my soul. Never would I have expected Ryne to be so cruel. There's no excuse for it. He doesn't love me, not like I love him, because if he did, he would never reject me like this. He would never be so harsh. So cold. It's as if that bite changed him in every single way. The Ryne I knew is gone.

"Don't come back to the city." Then he shifts into his wolf form and disappears into the forest before I can say another word.

CHAPTER 3

I STORM BACK to the camp and into Callum's tent. Nico is gone, but Justin, Faye, and Callum are packing up.

"Where's Nico?" I demand.

"He ran after Ryne. We'll follow after we get this packed up. You should head to the panther city. You'll be safe there," Justin offers regretfully.

"Uh, no. I'm coming with you." Ryne may think he can boss me around all he wants, but I'm not the same girl I was when I came to the wolf city. I've been through it all, and I'm done taking orders.

Justin shakes his head. "No. Ryne doesn't want you to come back to the city. The Sanctuary is a good idea. You won't be safe with the wolves."

I snort. He thinks that Ryne is somehow looking out for me by keeping me away? Yeah, right.

"Why wouldn't I be safe?" I challenge.

He looks at me like it's obvious. "Because you're a lycan. You're not safe among wolves."

"Callum is going, and he's a lycan, remember? Besides, no one in that city knows what I really am except for you guys. I'm not going to be sent off just when I'm needed most." Everyone is quiet. I can't just let this go. I can't just leave them. "Where is Faye going?"

Faye juts her chin. "I'm going back to Drayton Hall. Those girls need my help. With Madame Delphine gone and Anders being Anders, things have to be a mess there."

I nod. That makes sense, but I'm surprised to see Faye doing something selfless. I figured she'd be taking the first chance she got to marry a beta, but since Ryne hasn't signed off on an early marriage to Justin yet, maybe she's just saving face. "That's a good idea. I'll help you." A thought springs to mind. "I'm not totally opposed to the panthers, you know. We can sneak girls out of the city and get them to The Sanctuary."

I expect an argument, for the old Faye to surface, but she gives me a conspiratorial grin and nudges me. "I like it. Who knew you and I would team up one day?"

I force a grin. I'm still reeling over Ryne being so angry with me, but I have to pretend like everything is fine. If I let on that Ryne doesn't want me around because he's mad at me, then they really won't let me come with.

Justin meets my eyes. "Look, I know it's hard to

understand right now, but Ryne cares about you and would want to keep you safe. The panthers will be able to provide that."

Faye snorts. "He also said he never wants to see her again. You call that caring?"

Justin shakes his head. "He was just angry in the moment. He still loves her."

I don't tell him that Faye's right, that what Justin is calling protection and love is clearly rejection and betrayal. "Look, the only beta left in the claiming that I need to worry about is Anders, and he's going to be busy trying to either fight it out or suck up to Ryne once he returns. It's going to be a shock to the pack to have their alpha back. Let me at least come to Drayton so I can get a few girls out to The Sanctuary with me."

What I don't tell him is that I have no intention of staying with the panthers. No matter what, I'm staying in the wolf city. I have to see this through to the end, even if Ryne wants nothing to do with me. I can't help the claimed women if I'm not there. And if I have to be locked up on full moons with Callum, so be it.

Justin clenches his jaw. "Okay fine. But you leave as soon as you can. We won't tell Ryne that you came back with Faye. He'll be so busy with the pack that he won't worry about Drayton Hall at all. But get all the girls out. War is about to break out, and the last thing we need is to worry about what will happen to them, especially with Delphine gone. Poppy, you take them to The Sanctuary with you, and Faye, you go to my parents' house."

He briefly hesitates. "Unless you want to go with Poppy and the other girls to The Sanctuary. I would understand."

Faye grasps his hand. "No way. I'm sticking with you. And I'm not going to your parents' house. I'm staying at the manor until Ryne gives us his blessing."

I still can't tell if whatever is going on between them is real or not. Does Faye actually love him? That would explain why she's willing to give up The Sanctuary for him, but then again, she was willing to do just about anything to live an extravagant life as a beta wife. Maybe she's still hoping things will go back to the way they were, and if that's the case, it would be foolish to trust her.

Justin lets out a breath. "Okay. Let's go."

It's not exactly how I would've planned it, but at least I get to go back to the city. Once I'm there, I'll figure out my next steps.

And Ryne is just going to have to live with it.

FAYE and I stare up at the manor. My whole world changed three months ago when I was bitten, Joanna ran off with Grady, and Abi got sent to a mating house. In those following months, we managed to rescue a handful of claimed girls, but last I heard, Anders was making things worse for the ones left behind. That, and they were supposed to bring in more betas to court the remaining girls. Did that ever happen? Probably not without Ryne there to oversee it, but I'm not really sure.

Truth is, I have no idea what to expect when I walk through those doors.

"Did they ever bring in more betas?" I ask the question aloud.

Faye shakes her head. "I don't think so. They kept talking about it, but it never happened while I was there."

"Do we even know who's left?"

She shrugs. "That depends on who actually got sent to the mating houses."

"But Madame Delphine and Elle went to Chicago. Who's even running the manor now?"

"Vivien would be my best guess. But you forget, I've been out in the woods with you since you 'rescued' me." She rolls her eyes. "Things have probably changed."

Vivien has never been a fan of mine. I don't know how she's going to take to me telling her that we're sending all the girls to The Sanctuary.

"What's the plan?" I ask because I don't have one. I was so worried about getting back into the city that it never occurred to me what I would do when I got there. It's dark, the middle of the night, but there are still lights on.

Faye shrugs. "No clue. This was your plan, remember? Mine was just to get back to a warm bed and keep dating Justin until we can get married."

She tromps in front of me, and I scramble after her. I

don't like going in blind, but we are going to have to improvise anyway. We have no idea who is even here.

Faye bangs on the door until it opens, and a surprised Madame Vivien scrambles back with her hand on her chest. "Oh, thank goodness. I thought you were Anders."

Faye creases her eyebrows. "Why?"

Vivien wrings her hands but ushers us inside and locks the door behind us. "He was so upset that Delphine brought all the girls back here after the fight instead of sending them to the mating houses, but he had so many other things going on that he didn't push her. I literally haven't slept because I've been so worried that he's going to march in here and take them all."

She sinks down into a chair, and I notice the flash of red pinned to her dress.

It's a poppy.

CHAPTER 4

"YOU'RE PART OF THE RESISTANCE," I breathe out, suddenly so relieved I could cry.

She glances up. "And so are you. Do you really think Delphine would have women working for her that were not?" She stares at Faye for a second. "I didn't think you were in on it, though."

"I wasn't. But Justin and his family are, and I go where he goes. Speaking of. We've come to rescue the girls. Poppy is going to take them to The Sanctuary in Panther City."

Vivien shakes her head. "No. Delphine sent word earlier; she's on her way back. No one goes anywhere without her approval first."

"And if Anders shows up?"

Vivien pulls a wicked-looking knife from a sheath on her side that I didn't even see. "We are all well-armed."

I wouldn't mind using that on Anders myself. I

thought that killing someone would irrevocably place a black stain on my soul, but if anything, I feel better now that Thorn is gone. Lighter. Freer. And I'm willing to kill bad people if it means saving the good ones, especially the ones I love. Ryne may not like it, but I'm glad I was the one to kill his father.

"Anders isn't the alpha," I state. "You don't have to worry about him anymore."

Madame Vivien stands and walks to the window, peering out into the darkness. "I would ask you where you two have been, but Madame Delphine already told me. As far as everyone else is concerned"—she turns back to us —"as far as *Anders* is concerned, you were kidnapped by a rogue group of lone wolves, the same wolves who also kidnapped Ryne, but you were all rescued by Justin and Nico. Nobody can know you've been around the lycan, is that understood?"

"Oh, we understand perfectly," Faye agrees. "And we've already talked through our story with Justin and Nico ten times over on the way back to the city. You don't need to worry about us."

I nod along, but a prickle of fear goes through me anyway. The wolves can't tell I'm lycan in this form, but what if I somehow give myself away since we're still so close to the previous full moon? I'll be dead before anyone can ask questions. Maybe this is why Ryne didn't want me to come back. At least, I know they can't smell the renewal on me since I washed it away the next morning. If it was something they could smell in this form, Justin wouldn't have let me return.

"There's a large bounty for any information that could lead to the capture of our alpha king's killer." She gives us a hard look, me in particular. "Do you happen to know anything about that?"

My mouth pops open, but Faye beats me to it. "Of course not, but we can't say we're unhappy he's dead, now can we?"

My mind flashes to the night the king roughed up Faye, the way the light in her eyes dimmed after spending time alone with him. Maybe she really can be trusted. But I've been betrayed by people I love too many times to trust anyone at all. I'm keeping my guard up.

"Yes, I happen to agree with you, but I just wanted to make sure you knew that the lycan who killed King Tremaine has a target on his *or her* back now."

I'm not about to confess it was me. Madame Vivien probably knows I'm a lycan, but I can't be sure. If she were to also find out I killed the king, who's to say she wouldn't turn me in for the bounty? She may be with the Resistance, but I'm not sure that means she's on my side. She blames me for her friend's death and could still want retaliation beyond all those grueling workouts she put me through last spring. I guess I'll just have to get used to walking around with a target on my back and hope that nobody stabs it.

"You two take Poppy's old room and go on to bed."

I want to stay and ask questions, wondering who's still here, if more betas ever showed up to court, how we can get more women out, and what Anders has been up to lately. I open my mouth to speak because I can't stand not knowing, but Madame Vivien shoots me an exasperated look and points to the stairs. "We'll talk more later. Right now, it'd be best if you went upstairs."

Because she's expecting Anders, and even though I'm not her favorite person, she's still trying to protect me. I should appreciate it, but I'm tired of other people telling me to go away as a form of protection.

I swallow hard, not wanting to leave, but I do as my house mother asks anyway. I'm not the same girl I was when she last saw me, not by a million miles, but I'm exhausted. It's been several days and nights of pure hell, months of living in a tent, and the thought of sleeping in a real bed makes me want to cry with happiness. Faye must feel the same way because she's up the stairs before me.

"I'm taking a shower first," she announces.

Now *that* sounds even better than sleeping right now. I follow her to the shared showers, and we quickly clean ourselves under the hot pelt of water before changing into clean pajamas and crawling into our beds. Seeing Faye in my friends' old bed is wrong, but I don't argue with it. My head barely hits the pillow before sleep claims me.

BANG! I bolt upright and immediately go into defensive mode. *Bang! Bang! Bang!*

"Faye, wake up," I hiss, but she's already awake.

"I'm not going down there."

Someone is pounding on the manor's front door, and from the sounds of it, they're eager to get inside.

"Well, I'm not hiding up here," I say back. I dig under the mattress and find the dagger I hid there ages ago, still waiting for me, then run for the door.

"Are you sure that's a good idea?" She tries to block me. "Not many people even know we're up here. That could be a good thing. Maybe we should hide?" Faye never struck me as a coward, but then again, she was never one to protect others either.

"You hide. I'm leaving." And with that, I throw open the door and sprint down the stairs, taking them two at a time, ignoring the heads peeking from the other doorways and the whispers that follow.

"Madame Vivien, let me in or face the consequences." I hear Anders call through the locked front door.

She's standing in the darkened room, the shine of that nasty knife gleaming silver in her hand.

"He's going to find a way in either way," I whisper. "You know he will."

"There's been a change of plans," he calls again. "Either open this door, or I'll break it down."

He starts banging again and then goes quiet. Eerily so. That's when the window shatters, and a large gray wolf lands in the center of the room. He growls as he turns on us, and then he pauses, his eyes zeroing in on me. It's the perfect opportunity for Madame Vivien to strike.

She sees her opening and slashes her knife at his neck. I take advantage of the moment and plunge my dagger into his side. He howls and flings Vivien into the wall with his giant paw. She crumples to the ground, her knife still in hand.

He turns on me, blood dripping from his neck and ribs, and bares his razor-sharp teeth. I back up a few feet. I don't have any good angles to strike from, and I wish that I had a sword instead of a measly dagger. He lunges for me, but before he can get his jaws around my neck, two more wolves leap through the window and knock him down.

He scrambles back to his feet and growls at them.

Then they all turn into very large naked men. I flick my eyes up so I don't have to look at them. It's Justin and Nico who've come to save me, and my heart drops a little that it isn't Ryne. Hope can be so cruel.

"We just rescued her, and now you're trying to kill her?" Nico asks, breathing hard.

Anders presses a hand to his side, blood seeping out between his fingers. "She attacked me first."

"Looks like she was just protecting herself like we taught her to. Good job, Poppy," Justin adds.

Footsteps scramble down the stairs, and Faye flings herself into Justin's arms as if they haven't seen each other in ages. It's beyond ridiculous. Anders just glares at all of us.

"Fine, protect your pets. I didn't come here for them anyway. When Ryne finally dies, and I become alpha, I'll kill her. You better pick another wife, Nico."

"I'm not interested in any of the others," Nico lies. We both know there's nothing between us, that our sham engagement was never about love, but right now I'm so grateful to Nico that I could kiss him. It wouldn't mean anything, but to see him stand up to his own father for me?

It's what Ryne should've done . . .

Anders shrugs. "Suit yourself. Go gather the rest of the girls."

"For what?" Justin asks.

Anders pinches the bridge of his nose and squeezes his eyes shut. "We're losing good wolves from our pack because they want more women. They're threatening to leave for Chicago to fight for the position of alpha king since the position is still vacant. I'm going to release the rest of the girls to the mating houses as an incentive for them to stay. In addition, I'm sending men out to the surrounding villages to gather more women. Then, hopefully, we can keep the pack together."

"You can't do that," I shout.

He rolls his eyes. "I can, and I will."

"It's not your place. You're not the alpha." Justin glares.

"Not yet. But I am second in command, and until

Ryne returns, I'm in charge. I'm only doing what's best for the pack."

Justin and Nico exchange glances, and a grin spreads over Nico's face. He turns around, unlocks the front door, and turns back to the group. He crosses his arms and smirks at Anders. "Suit yourself, but I'm not helping you anymore, *Father*."

Anders bears down on him, growling. "I am in charge, and you will obey me, *son*."

Nico chuckles. "No, I won't. You have no control in my life anymore."

The door flings open suddenly, and we all spin. Ryne stands there, breathing heavily. He's clean and has on fresh clothes, and his hair is brushed back into a low ponytail. I want to go to him, but I can't. Not after what he said to me. Not after what he *did*.

He glances around the room, taking in everything. His eyes stop at mine and narrow, but he doesn't say anything.

"What's going on?" he asks Anders.

"Ryne, you're looking healthy. I thought you were left for dead."

"I survived."

"I see. Well, the men are hungry for fresh meat, so I came to get it for them."

"These girls are not yours for the taking, Anders. They are still going through the process of matching with a beta. You cannot take that from them."

"Oh, please. The betas have already made their

choices. Cade is dead. Justin wants Faye. I'll back down to let Nico have Poppy, considering you don't want her, and she's probably used goods after what those lone wolves did with her." His lip curls as he looks at me and then at his son. "I don't want any of the ones who are left, so I'm backing out of the claiming this year."

"And your point?" Ryne seethes between clenched teeth.

"Give the men what they want."

"That's not your call. Remember, I'm your alpha."

"Not for long."

Ryne takes a step forward. "You're challenging me?"

Anders snorts. "No. I have bigger ambitions than just that. If you won't be reasonable and give your own men what they deserve, then I'm going to Chicago to fight for alpha king myself." He puffs up his chest. "Then I'll come down and remove you from your post, and the Carolina Pack will run the way it's supposed to."

He shoulder-checks Ryne as he stalks away, turning into a wolf as soon as he clears the doorway. Nico and Justin stare at Ryne. Justin's lips are thin, and Nico looks like he's about ready to murder his father himself.

"No. We aren't going to chase him down," Ryne announces. "Let him go to Chicago and get himself killed. Good riddance. Nico, stay here and protect the girls tonight. I'll send some more betas over to help. Justin, come with me."

"What are we going to do?" Justin questions.

"We're going to take control of the pack once more

and try to keep as many men as we can from following Anders to Chicago."

"Aren't you going up there to fight for alpha king?"

Just the thought of it makes me feel ill. Ryne's not weak, but he nearly died twice in the last few days, and he might not be in a position to battle for that title right now. Luckily, he shakes his head. "I'll worry about the alpha king later. Izaak is strong enough to win the throne, and we already trust him. If he fails, however, and if it ends up going to someone we can't trust, well, only then will I fight for the crown."

It's something we talked about a lot, something I wanted for him, and he knows it. His eyes meet mine again, but once again, he has no words for me. He and Justin leave without another word or even a backward glance. Nico strides over to Vivien and helps her to her feet. She's shaky but otherwise unharmed.

"What now?" I ask.

Vivien stands tall. "Now, we go back to normal."

CHAPTER 5

I TURN that word over and over in my head, trying to make sense of it. *Normal.* It seems like a joke that we could go back to normal around here, but then again, nothing about the last nine months could be described as normal. Anders brutally murdering my sister and then forcing me to come here in her place wasn't normal. The forced breeding in order to keep the pack growing and competing to marry a beta wolf wasn't normal. Falling in love with the alpha, a man I should hate, wasn't normal. And becoming a lycan certainly wasn't normal. I never would've guessed that I could thrive as a lycan, but during that last renewal, I'd finally been able to take back my control, to protect myself, to be strong, and to fight.

And I won. I killed King Thorn Tremaine.

All that, and I am now expected to get prettied up and pretend as if none of it happened?

Because that's exactly what we did after we went

back upstairs, only this time with Faye as my roommate instead of Charlotte or Joanna or Abi. Maybe for Vivien, this is normal. This is the way things have been her entire life, but for me, this seems like a cosmic joke.

Faye smirks at me from across the room, smoothing out her skirts. "What are you going to tell the other girls?"

I adjust my own skirts and study myself in the mirror. I feel like so much has changed, *I've changed*, but I look the exact same as I did when I left here. How can that possibly be? "Just what Madame Vivien requested. That we were captured by lone wolves, and then we were rescued. Nobody needs to know anything else."

And if Faye brings up my being a lycan to the wrong person, I'm as good as dead. I'm expecting her to blackmail me with that right about now, but instead, she rolls her eyes. "Aren't you forgetting what happened at your sham wedding? You confessed to being Ryne's fated mate. Everyone knows about you two now. And not only that, I know you're no innocent virgin anymore."

Blood drains from my face. I hadn't thought about that. One of the rules for the claiming is that none of the girls are allowed to lose their virtue before marriage, and if they do, they'll be sent to the mating houses. And now that everyone knows about Ryne, they're going to treat me differently, especially the betas.

"Pretty sure they're going to think neither of us are virgins, considering we were supposedly taken by lone wolves," I state. "But none of that matters anymore.

We're not actually going through with the claiming, and it's not for another three months anyway. There's going to be a new king, a better one, and Ryne is going to make changes around here. And don't forget we're supposed to be leaving for The Sanctuary soon."

"Not me. I'm marrying Justin."

So she says, but I'm still not sure if those two are the real deal.

"Well, some of us will be leaving, whether or not we're still virgins."

"I guess we'll see what happens but I'm not counting on that plan."

I don't say anything more because she's right and also because I don't want to leave the city either. Running away isn't going to solve whatever went wrong between me and Ryne. And besides, I need to stick around in case he needs me. He's acting like he isn't infected with the lycanthrope virus, but I know, come this next full moon, something is going to change. Something big. I'm just not sure what yet.

We go down to breakfast, making a dramatic entrance as is Faye's way. And she's right. Everyone swarms us with questions and suspicions. They especially want to know all about my interactions with Ryne, of which I lie and pretend there are few. The whole time, Faye has this knowing smirk on her face like she could spill my secrets at any moment. And maybe she will.

There aren't many original claimed girls left. So

many have died, and the ones who are still alive aren't all here. Charlotte is off with the lycans, who think it's okay to turn humans against their will, and now so is Joanna because Grady believes it's the safest place for them. Faye's distillery friend Joy is still here, though she's a shell of the girl she was before, and I wonder what happened to her. Katelyn was sent to the mating house at the last festival, as was Emma. My stomach twists thinking about the others who've been at the mating houses for even longer, like Abi. Especially Abi. We saved Alyssa, Bailey, Harlow, and Blair for the panther city, so they're safe for now. Samantha is here and is probably still top of the leaderboard. She and Raven look like they've become best friends in the months since I've been away, and I wonder if they'd be willing to leave all this for The Sanctuary. Joy is still here. And then there's me and Faye.

Five women.

Five women, but what of the betas who were supposed to choose a bride?

Cade is dead.

Grady is long gone.

Anders left for Chicago—thank goodness. I hope he dies there.

Justin has apparently picked Faye to be his future wife.

Nico might still be courting after our botched wedding, though people seem to think we're still engaged. He'll forever be heartbroken over Nova–his fated mate who was murdered by his own father—and I don't think Ryne will make him get married. I'm certainly not going to marry him.

So why are we even still here?

A feeling of hopelessness settles over me as I eat the first decent meal I've had in months. Not even sugary pancakes can cheer me up. I don't know what to do next. Do I really leave the city and take the girls with me? Do I leave Ryne? Or do I stay here and pretend that things are back to normal when I know they'll never be normal again?

Samantha settles in next to me, nudging me on the shoulder. "We all know about the Resistance," she whispers low, "and we're on your side. We're going to get through this together."

I turn to meet her bright amber eyes, this girl who I've barely spoken two words to, this girl who I thought I had little in common with, who is now nodding and giving me a knowing look of encouragement. She reminds me to remember how far I've come. I can't back down now. I can't give up. There are still so many lives at stake, and just because women are in the mating houses now doesn't mean they aren't important. If anything, saving them is more crucial than saving the girls in the manor.

"I need to talk to Ryne," I announce, standing up.

Everyone quiets and stares at me.

"I'm afraid the alpha doesn't take requests,"

Madame Vivien says, arching her thin brow over her morning cup of coffee, "not even from his fated mate."

But before I can argue with her, the door swings open, and everyone holds in a collective gasp. I almost expect it to be Ryne—but it's better.

It's Elle.

CHAPTER 6

I RUSH OUT of my seat and fling my arms around her. She holds me tight for a minute before letting go, keeping me at arm's length to study me. "Are you okay?" she asks softly. Her eyes carry dark circles and a haunted look—her eyes have seen too much.

I nod, but my face probably betrays me because she purses her lips.

"What happened in Chicago?" I question.

She shakes her head, her mouth trembling in a grief-stricken way that's nothing like the girl I know. "Nothing good. My father is dead."

I let out a little gasp as pain rakes through me. Pain for Elle, for the Resistance, for Ryne, for myself, for all of us. Izaak being dead was not in our plans.

"My family went into hiding," she continues, "but I couldn't leave Delphine alone. She needed help getting back safely with..." She falters.

"With what?"

But before she answers, a girl I don't recognize pushes past her. "Is there food? I'm starving."

Elle steps aside, and several more girls enter the room. They're of varying ages, and they're all beautiful like Elle, but other than that, none of them look alike. One has bright red curls and is covered in freckles, and another has long, shiny blonde hair. A third is short and curvy with warm brown skin and thick glasses. I can't figure out who they are. None of them are dressed like the girls from the villages, but where else could they be from?

Elle grins. "Ladies, meet the lunas."

We all go silent.

There are more than I expected, but if they are sent to Chicago from all the packs, that would make sense. I do a quick count. Including Elle, there are nine lunas. The youngest appears to only be about five years old, and the oldest seems my age. We have room for them here, of course, but no one knows what to expect from these new women. We all love Elle, so hopefully, they are just as wonderful as she is, but I've learned to never expect anything from anyone. Not that I'm worried about the little ones, but there are three who look like young women, and from my experience with the claiming, that could mean more women who hate me.

The redhead plops herself down next to Faye, takes her plate of food, and helps herself. A couple of the other girls do the same, several jumping in to help out the younger ones. The pretty blonde luna looks down her nose at Samantha. "What are you waiting for? We need food."

Samantha just gapes at her, but Faye leans forward with a nasty glint in her eye. "We're not your servants. Go into the kitchen and get it yourself." Then she snatches her plate back from the redhead.

The redhead whips her hand back and slaps Faye right across the face. "I am a luna and will not be talked to that way."

For a second, nothing happens—the sound of that slap seems to echo in the room, though I know it doesn't really.

Faye lifts her hand to her cheek, and then without warning, she growls and attacks the girl, both of them falling to the floor.

Elle rushes past me, Delphine on her heels. They yank the girls apart, but the girls are still glaring daggers at each other. Elle gets right in the redhead's face. "Violet, I know you were raised like a princess, but you're no better than these girls. You cannot slap them or demand things from them."

Violet sniffs. "They're humans, aren't they? They're only here to serve and make babies. Of course I'm better than them."

My jaw drops, and anger roils the pancakes in my stomach. I'll never forget what it felt like to be a helpless human in this world. Never.

Madame Delphine pushes past Elle. "You will not

speak of humans in that way. If you do not change your attitude, you are welcome to go back to Chicago and fend for yourself."

Violet's eyes widen. "You wouldn't dare send me back there. Chicago is dangerous for lunas right now."

"Try me."

Violet lets out an exasperated huff. "Fine. I'll be nice. But I am starving."

Something tells me she will not be nice. This is exactly why I need to talk to Ryne—these prejudices against humans need to be corrected. Especially now that Izaak is dead and the Resistance has been cut off at the knees. Ryne's the only one who can demand change around here, so where is he?

"Elle, why don't you show them where the kitchen is so they can help themselves to food? Then get them set up in rooms and see if Vivien can find clothes for them. We'll work the rest out later." Madame Delphine turns on me, her lips thinning. "Poppy, we need to talk."

She brushes past me, and I follow her to her office.

Madame Delphine shuts the door and leans against her desk. She brushes the hair away from her aging face with shaky hands. "Please tell me what happened. I've heard the rumors, of course, but I want to hear everything from you. I know Thorn is dead, but they're saying Ryne didn't do it."

I shake my head. "That's because I did."

She gasps. "Well, that complicates things, doesn't it? I want the whole story."

She sinks into a chair, and I sit on the couch and spill everything. From renewing as a lycan, to killing Thorn, to accidentally biting Ryne.

"Thank goodness he's alive, but he's not talking to me. I don't know what will happen to him on the full moon."

"That's a lot to process." She offers a small grin. "I'll talk to Ryne this afternoon about his pigheadedness. You should be staying with him at his home, not here." She tilts her head at me, her eyes looking me up and down. "Have you two been intimate?"

"I'm useful here," I blurt out. "I want to stay at the manor."

"Okay." But her knowing eyes catch it all, and once again I'm prickling with shame. I gave Ryne everything, and he left me in the wilds.

"What's happening in Chicago?" I ask.

She sighs. "It's a bloodbath. When we left, they were still fighting to be the alpha king. And new wolves arrive every day, wanting to fight for the throne." She swallows hard. "They're willing to fight to the death. When Elle's father died yesterday morning in battle, we knew we had to get out of there."

"I still can't believe it," I whisper. "I thought he was going to win."

"We all did," Madame Delphine says. "The Resistance was counting on it."

My heart is breaking for our cause, but most of all, it's sinking for Elle. I can tell she's trying to be strong, to act like she's okay, but I know what it feels like to have your world ripped apart like that. She's not okay. "And the lunas?"

"They were vulnerable. Wolves kept coming to their academy to try and steal them away, thinking being married to a luna would make them stronger for the throne."

I shake my head, horrified to imagine it. Most of those lunas are far too young to be married. And to be married to someone who only wants them to strengthen their position?

It's wrong.

"So we offered them refuge with us. At least here they won't be used as pawns. They all trust Elle, and Elle trusts Ryne, so they agreed to come with us."

"They aren't very nice."

Her lips thin, and she lets out a long sigh. "From the time they were babies, they've been raised to think they're better than other women. Each will be married off to the most powerful alphas in the kingdom. They have been waited on hand and foot and never told they were wrong. The only person they ever feared was Thorn, and you can imagine why."

"But Elle's not like that," I argue.

"Elle is a special soul, but she was also raised by a wonderful beta family." Delphine stands. "All of these girls were raised in the academy. Their tutelage was overseen by the king himself. They're not as lucky as Elle."

I nod in understanding.

"I'm going to see Ryne. Would you like to come with me?" Delphine asks.

I'm out of my chair before she can change her mind.

She chuckles. "Let's go."

THERE ARE things Ryne and I need to talk about besides our messy relationship. As much as I want to demand he take me back, my heart isn't what's most important right now. Saving the women in the mating houses is.

We're driven over to Ryne's house by a new driver, a burly wolf shifter with a mean expression. I keep expecting to see Knox's kind eyes watching me through the rearview mirror, but of course, Knox is long gone. I would be happy for him and Charlotte if they hadn't sided with Laik and Wanda. I wonder where they're at now, what they're doing, and if they're going to attack the Carolina Pack soon. Laik's people have gone rogue, biting humans to build their army, and some of my best friends willingly went with them. What does this mean for the Resistance? Delphine and I don't even get a chance to talk about that in detail, but I explain the basics despite there being so much going on at the moment that I can't even think straight.

The car pulls to a stop in front of Ryne's beautiful white home, and I swallow back my nerves. Delphine doesn't bother to knock; she walks right inside the alpha's home, calling out to her son.

Ryne rounds the corner, barely giving me a second glance. He gives his mother a kiss on the cheek. "I was just leaving. I can come down to the manor later."

Madame Delphine isn't having it. "You don't have time for your mother?"

I want to add "and your fated mate" to that sentence but keep my mouth shut.

"I'm needed in the villages." He finally meets my gaze but breaks away quickly. "There's no time. We can talk later, Poppy."

"We're coming with you," I demand. It's been nine months since I've seen my parents, since I left little Evan and my father without saying goodbye. I never thought I'd see them again. This is my chance.

"No." Ryne's tone is sharp. Final. How quickly he forgot that we fought together out in the wilds and even against his father. I have just as much right to go.

"Which village?" I beg. I don't know if I want him to say Northwest or not. I'd give anything to see them again, but I don't want them to be in any kind of trouble.

"Southeast," he says. "There's a rumor that they were visited by lycans at the last moon."

We both know what that means. People were turned. Laik must be working with more lycans who share his mindset. Ryne doesn't stick around to address the horror in his mother's eyes.

He tears out the door, and I chase after him. "We

can ride with you," I call out. "Explain your plan on the way. Maybe we can help."

Ryne turns back. "You'll only get in the way. You're not even supposed to be here."

Delphine marches up to him, getting right in his face. "I know you're angry with Poppy, but that doesn't give you the right to talk to her that way or boss her around like that. This sounds like a problem for the Resistance, so we will be joining you, whether you like it or not."

Ryne gives me a glare but nods to his mother. "Just don't get in the way."

CHAPTER 7

WE FOLLOW him out the front door, and I try to ignore the sting of his continued rejections. Right now, I need to be less concerned with our happily-ever-after and more concerned with the things that need to change.

With Thorn dead, there is no reason to have the mating houses or the claiming anymore. Ryne promised he'd get rid of them, and I have every intention of making sure he sticks to his word.

Two trucks are waiting out front now, both beds filled with wolf shifter men, some in their human forms and some more comfortable in their wolves. Ryne climbs into the driver's seat of one truck, and Nico is already driving the other. Madame Delphine climbs in with Ryne, leaving me with Nico.

I don't hesitate to join him—I'm not getting left behind—but I am nervous. Nico and I haven't been alone since I abandoned him at our sham wedding.

Nico gives me a tight grin and puts the truck into gear, following Ryne down the street.

Neither one of us says anything for several minutes.

"I'm sorry I lied to you about the wedding."

Nico sighs. "I wish you would've been honest with me about the whole thing, but I get it. And we both knew there was no romantic love between us. At this point, I'm not sure I'm going to take a bride, and I'm happier that way. Someday, when the pain is gone, I might. But for now, I'm going to focus on being a warrior beta."

I want to argue with him about not taking a bride, which means forcing one more girl to go to a mating house, but if Ryne sticks to his word, then it won't matter. Besides, who am I to deny Nico his wishes?

I stare out the window as the city drops away. "Thank you for not hating me."

He reaches over and squeezes my hand. "I may not have loved you, but I do care for you and your wellbeing. I promised Nova I would look out for you, and I intend to keep that promise. At least, until Ryne's speaking to you again. Then he can look out for you." He chuckles, but I don't see the humor in it.

"You really think he'll forgive me?"

"He's alive, isn't he?"

"Yeah."

"Then he'll forgive you. We can't stay away from our fated mates, no matter how badly we want to."

I clench my fists. "I don't want him to come back to me because he feels obligated."

"He won't. It'll be because he loves you and wants you around. Just give him some time."

I roll my window down and let my hand hang in the wind. I don't know how much more my heart can take. "That's what everyone keeps saying, but I just want to fast forward to the part where he loves me again."

"I know."

Then I realize how selfish I'm being. Here I am, whining about how Ryne isn't talking to me, and Nico's fated mate is dead. Sometimes I marvel at my own stupidity. We need to talk about something else.

"What do you know about what happened to the village?"

"Not much. A man came into the city today, claiming that lycans came and took his wife. We're going to investigate."

"Where's the man?"

"He's staying with Shauna and Amos for now."

"Do you think the whole Carolina Pack will join the Resistance or not?"

"Of course not, but many will once things become public. Ryne's just waiting for the alpha king to be named before making his move. It could be weeks or even months. Now that Izaak is dead, there's more chaos in Chicago than ever."

I hate the uncertainty of everything. Things seem even bleaker now than when Thorn was alpha king.

Between Laik and his turning people against their will to the lack of leadership among the wolves, nobody knows what's going to happen. Not for the first time, I long for the days before I was claimed. Where I climbed trees with Willow, worked the fields, and teased my little brother about the neighbor girl. At least, Evan is safe.

Or I hope he is. If Laik is attacking the villages, maybe he's not. Goosebumps rake across my skin. I'll have to see what I can do about checking on my family.

We drive for another thirty minutes and then pull into the middle of the village. People cautiously come out to look. I wave at a little girl who peers through a window. These people have likely never even seen a truck or a car before, and I know how disconcerting that can feel.

Ryne stops in front of us, and I scramble out of the car. Delphine and Nico join him as well. The other wolves stay in the truck bed.

A man approaches Ryne, hat in hand and head bowed.

Ryne speaks softly to him. "Tim from your village came to us and told us about his wife. He was pretty shaken up, so we decided to see what happened for ourselves."

The man runs a hand over his short hair. "They came out of nowhere, grabbed men, women, and children. Some from the same families, some not. We lost thirty-two souls that night."

My stomach drops. Thirty-two people.

Most of them will wish they were dead, come the next full moon, and not everyone will survive the renewal. I pray that those who do will be able to come to terms with their new lives. Except that's not why they were turned, was it? They're meant to be weapons against the shifters. They won't have a choice in the matter, especially the first time they become one of us. They'll be lost to the bloodlust.

"Do you think they're dead?" the man asks mournfully.

"We don't know," Ryne answers. "But we're leaving six wolves to protect your village and more come the next full moon. We're going to spend between now and then hunting down the lycan that took your people." He peers around at the shabby village and swallows. "Will you be able to feed and house the six?"

The man's face pales. "Yes, but what happened to the two wolves that were supposed to be protecting my village on the full moon?"

"They're gone," Ryne admits. "The lycans don't leave bodies behind, but as alpha, I can tell when anyone in my pack is cut away from me."

What must that be like? To have that kind of connection to so many people? It's no wonder Ryne has always put the needs of his pack above all else.

"I'm sorry to hear that. Thank you for coming and for bringing more wolves."

People have come out of their houses now and surround our company. I spot a girl about my age sneaking toward the front. She's pretty and graceful but has a scowl on her face. She catches me looking at her and waves me over.

"What's your name?" she asks in a whisper.

"Poppy, and yours?"

"Laura. Are you a claimed girl?"

"I am." My stomach hardens because I'm pretty sure I know where this conversation is going.

"I'm the only one from my village going at the next harvest moon. The women who help me prepare don't tell me anything other than to explain the pack hierarchy and proper behavior. But I don't know why I'm going to the city in the first place." She sneaks an awed look at Ryne then back to me. "I can't believe the alpha came all the way out here to help us. Is he going to be there when I get claimed?"

I want to give her some reassurance, but if I told her the truth, what would she do? Would she try to run? Would it help her to know or hurt her? I bite my lip and consider. "Listen carefully," I say. "Things should be better by the time you arrive, but if they're not, you need to remember that the other claimed women are not your enemy."

Confusion sparks in her eyes. "Why would they be my enemy?"

I take her hand and squeeze it tight. "That's the point. They're not, and don't let anyone make you believe differently. You got that?"

She nods once.

"I wish I could tell you more." I suck in a breath. The claiming is in less than three months. I can't believe it's almost time for another one. "Honestly, if your whole family can run and get to the panther city down south, they have a sanctuary there, and you could—"

"Panthers?" She drops my hand and steps back. If she looked confused before, she's positively bewildered now. And unnerved. I've scared her, and I want to kick myself for that. Of course, she doesn't know about the panthers. I should've just kept my mouth shut.

"That's enough," Ryne cuts in. "It's time to go."

He grabs my upper arm and marches me back to the truck, setting me in the front seat next to him. There aren't any shifters coming back with us, so he must have sent them out after the lycans and left his six to protect the village. My mouth flattens into a thin line. If he'd kept his promise from the beginning and actually protected this village properly, none of those innocent humans would've been taken.

My relationship with Ryne has been complicated from day one.

I love him, and I hate him.

Both emotions shouldn't exist together, but they do, and right now, I'm ready to let them out.

CHAPTER 8

"SO WHAT'S THE PLAN, ALPHA?" I ask the question without an ounce of civility. Talking to Laura and seeing the hope in her eyes quickly slip into fear has surfaced the anger I've been holding inside. "Are you going to let those people fend for themselves out there in the wilds with Laik's crew, or are you going to hunt them down and kill them all?"

Ryne's long fingers tighten on the steering wheel as he maneuvers us back to the road. We're on the complete opposite side of the wolf city from my village. Northwest isn't accessible by car because of the river with its crumbling bridge, and my heart twists as I recall the times I made it over that bridge or across that river, but never once to see my family.

"If you must know, I gave them a no-kill order for newly bitten," he says at last, and then he adds, "at least until the full moon when we can see what we're dealing with."

"Being a lycan isn't what you think."

"The bite is the one thing that can kill my people," he growls. "What would you have me do?"

"Have mercy," I state. "And are you forgetting that you're—"

He cuts me off. "Don't say it. Don't you dare."

I throw my hands up. "Fine, stay in denial, but it won't change what happened to you or that you were bitten too. Trust me, I should know."

He turns to glare at me, and I glare back. He's incredibly sexy when he's angry, and I have half a mind to do something about that, to bring him back to me, back to us, to remind him why he loves me so much. And just forget about all the bad blood between us.

But I have to be strong. What I'm about to say is far more important.

I inhale a steadying breath and let it out slowly. "Remember when we were back in the tent, and we talked about all the ways we could fix the city once your father was dead?" I don't wait for him to answer because, of course, he remembers. "It's time to start doing those things, Ryne, beginning with shutting down the mating houses."

No more forced breeding. No more rape. No more claiming. He owes me and the girls that much.

Ryne doesn't say anything for a long time, and my already broken heart begins to shatter because I know him. *I know him.* And if he's not agreeing with me, it's because he's changed his mind.

"Say it," I snap. "I want to hear you say it."

He sighs heavily. "It's not so simple."

"It is, though." All he has to do is say no more. His wolves have to listen to him. They don't have a choice. "That's what being the alpha means. You're in control."

"Being an alpha means so much more than control, Poppy. Just because I'm not making these changes now doesn't mean I never will. I just barely returned to my pack, and if I start making massive changes right now, it will be worse for everyone. Especially the girls. I'm going to do it when it's safest."

"You're waiting for it to be safe?" I laugh bitterly. "Take a look around, Ryne. It's never going to be safe. This world is a terrible place for humans, and what you're doing is making it so much worse. The lycans wouldn't hate you so much if there weren't mating houses and slaves. Maybe none of those people would've been kidnapped on the full moon if you'd made the necessary changes already."

"Don't pin what Laik did on me." His voice is low and murderous. Maybe I deserve that, but he's being completely unreasonable.

"I know you weren't there that night, and I know Anders was acting as stand-in alpha at the time, but tell me why I never saw wolves patrolling my village during the full moons. Was it all a lie? Because the other lycans told me that the humans were never their enemies or their targets. It was always you guys."

"We were the enemies? Have you already forgotten what just happened during the last full moon?" he seethes. "And what about all the other people who were bitten by lycans? And are you forgetting about yourself? About what Laik did to you?"

"I could never forget what happened to me and the terror of becoming a lycan, but that's not the point I'm making."

We sit in silence for a long minute, and it nearly kills me not to say anything, but it's his turn to explain himself. And he needs to because, as far as I can tell, he's a hypocrite. If I thought my heart was broken before, it's utterly decimated now.

"It's my job to protect my pack," he says. "You have no idea the pressure of that. I do protect the villages when it's needed, but it wasn't needed for a long time. You're right. I didn't have men out patrolling on full moons until recently, but now that there's been an attack on a village, I've got more men out in the field than I've ever had before." He's driving faster. Too fast. His anger is fueling the truck's speed. I grab onto my seat belt and squeeze. "I've got young wolves out there as we speak, wolves far younger than I've ever had to send out before. Many of them are searching the wilds and putting their lives at risk. How do you think that makes me feel?"

Part of me wants to hit him. "How dare you make this all about yourself. It's not about how you feel. What about the feelings of the humans who got bitten or lost their loved ones? What about how the claimed feel?" I'm squeezing the seatbelt so damn tight that it's practically biting into my hands, but I don't let up, and he doesn't slow the truck. "And what about *me*?"

"Everything I ever did was for my pack before you came along and got in the way."

He says it like I'm some kind of stain, like I'm not the love of his life but the curse of it. All those tender touches. All those kisses. The way we burned together in the dark of night inside that tent. Our whispered "I love yous" and the stolen glances. All of it comes tumbling down around me.

"I can't believe you would go back on your word like this. I thought you cared about what happens to the women."

"I'll set everything right when I can, once I know who the alpha king is and how to position our pack. And before you tell me to go fight for king, I'm not leaving my pack to do that. Not when they need me most."

Tears burn in my eyes, blurring my vision.

"Don't cry," he says softly, a shadow of my lover returning to me. But it's only a shadow—not the real thing.

"Don't worry. I won't give you any more of my tears," I whisper back. "I've already given you far too many."

He winces, and we don't say anything more after that. I stare out the window as the world passes by, so completely broken inside at the hands of the one person who was supposed to hold me together. Ryne was supposed to choose me. To love me the most. But once again, he's not the devoted fated mate. He's the alpha wolf putting the needs of his pack above all else, even when it's wrong. *Because this is wrong.* I made excuses for him before because of his father, but even with Thorn gone, things are still the same. He'll never be willing to risk his pack for the humans. I truly thought I could trust Ryne after everything we've been through, but it turns out I was wrong.

He drives me straight to the manor.

"One more thing," he says as he slows to a stop, but I don't wait for him to finish. I tear from the truck, slamming the door behind me, and sprint toward the manor. As far as I'm concerned, he had plenty of time to talk during the last half hour of our pained silence. I'm not sticking around another minute to let him break me more than he already has.

Ryne and I are officially done.

CHAPTER 9

A PILLOW HITS MY HEAD. "Get up." Faye's voice is too loud. I promised myself I wouldn't cry anymore, but I failed, crying myself to sleep last night. How could I not? I still can't believe what Ryne is doing. And how could I have been so fooled? I saw a man in him who didn't actually exist, not when it mattered anyway.

"What's the point?" I mutter and use the pillow she hit me with to cover my eyes.

She rips the pillow away. "The point is that Madame Delphine said we have to get up and get dressed. The betas are coming, and she wants it to look like everything is normal."

"Betas? You mean Justin and Nico? They already know everything, so who cares?"

She grabs my arm and pulls. "It's not just Justin and Nico. Madame Delphine won't say what's going on, only that wolves are coming here who aren't part of the Resistance, so the manor and everyone in it have to look normal."

I sit up and rub my eyes. "Normal?" I snort. "With only six of us claimed girls left? Hardly."

"It's not just us anymore. The lunas are here as well."

"They aren't part of the claiming." I point out the obvious. Those girls still act like the world owes them something just for being born, and it's getting old fast.

"You think that'll stop them from snatching up our men? You are lucky you're fated to Ryne. I still have no guarantees with Justin."

I roll my eyes, but as I look at Faye with her little pout and troubled expression, I realize she's being serious. She's actually worried about the lunas stealing her man. "Justin loves you," I whisper. "I wouldn't worry about that. And Ryne and I are finished. Fated mate means nothing to Ryne."

She means more to Justin than I do to Ryne.

Faye stands and pulls her dress down a little so her cleavage sticks out more. She assesses herself in the mirror for another full minute until she's satisfied, and then she grabs a dress out of the closet and tosses it to me. "You really believe that, huh? Fine. Whatever. But Ryne will be here with them, and this will show him what he's missing. Put it on, and let's go see what all the fuss is about."

I put on the dress only because I don't want to argue with her anymore. It's fitted tight in the bodice and way shorter than anything I'd normally wear, but she has a point about showing Ryne what he's missing.

She glances up at the clock then returns to the mirror yet again to smooth out her already silky auburn hair. Faye has a way of looking gorgeous under every circumstance, even when we were in the wilds. I thought maybe she'd have a facial scar from when Abi beat the snot out of her, but she healed up perfectly and went right back to looking like a future beta wife. "Sit. If we skip breakfast, I can do your hair and makeup."

I don't want to skip breakfast, but I oblige and watch her work. We don't talk. It's not like we're magically friends now, and I don't know what we'd say even if we were. We don't know why Ryne is showing up with a bunch of betas who aren't part of the Resistance, but I'm sure it's all for the good of his pack. I nearly roll my eyes. That's the only thing he cares about, apparently.

Faye loops her arm through mine when it's time to go downstairs. "We're friends now," she says as if able to read my thoughts. "Don't think too hard about it, okay? People can be enemies and then become friends. It happens. It's called character growth."

I snort but don't correct her and don't tug my arm away. It's surreal, and I don't trust it, but at least I'm not alone. I miss Joanna, though. Fiercely. I miss her almost as much as I miss Willow. And then there's my family and Abi—I don't think I can take another loss. Becoming friends with Faye puts me at risk for more pain.

We hit the entryway just as the door is opening. Justin is the first to enter, followed closely by Callum. It's strange seeing Callum here, especially with his head now buzzcut to look like a claimed boy. Three more men that I don't know enter, and Ryne is the last inside. Justin makes a beeline for Faye, swinging her around. She giggles and holds tight to him.

Callum comes up and gives me a kiss on the cheek. "Nice dress," he mutters and backs away, giving Ryne a glance, who glares at him.

Good.

"You let a claimed boy near these women?" One of the new wolves questions his alpha.

"I do not," Ryne says, and Callum blanches, stepping back against the far wall. Very few people know what he really is, and the last thing he needs to do is draw attention to himself. Still, I can't shake the image of Ryne's possessive glare when Callum kissed my cheek. Maybe there's something to Faye's plan of making Ryne jealous. At this point, I'll do anything if it means getting through to him. He needs to honor his word, to be the man I know he can be, the man he talked of being in the wilds.

Vivien enters from a side door. "What are you two doing out here? You should be with the other girls out on the lawn."

Faye grabs my hand and pulls me away from the men. Two of them are checking me out. Maybe Faye knows what she's doing. Not that I'd give Ryne the time of day unless he does what he promised.

We join the other four claimed girls. I can't believe it's come down to just us. Elle and the three lunas around our age are here as well, including my least favorite, Violet. I stride up to Elle.

"What's going on?"

She crosses her arms and glares at the men as they descend the steps onto the lawn. "Nothing good. Ryne thinks he's doing the right thing, but this is a stupid distraction."

"What is he doing?"

But before she can answer, Ryne waves us all closer. Delphine and Vivien have joined them.

"Ladies, it's been a rough year. We've lost too many girls. Cade died in battle. Grady and Joanna have run off. Nico lost his fated, and Anders has left our pack for Chicago. It's not been fair to you. In an effort to make things a bit better, I'm bringing in three more betas."

This was talked about before I was bitten, but it never came to fruition, and it's not a solution. It's the same old thing, and my fists ball tightly as I glare at Ryne. He doesn't even flinch.

"That's enough for each of us," Samantha hisses next to me.

I can do the math as well, but it only twists the knife in deeper because it looks like Ryne has written me off once and for all. So that's it? He proclaims his love for me, we sleep together, and then it's back to the claiming for me? I'm a lycan now. Sure, I can hide what I am during the full moons for now with careful planning, but that won't happen if I get married off to the wrong guy.

Ryne chuckles. "What Samantha said is only partially true. It wouldn't be a good claiming if there wasn't a little competition."

"What are you talking about?" I ask, forgetting that I vowed to never speak to him again.

"The lunas who are of age," he says, pointing at the three of them and Elle, "will be dating the betas as well. In the end, the betas will choose. If they choose you humans, then you don't have to worry about the mating houses. If they choose a luna, then . . ." He lets his words trail off.

"A luna doesn't have to agree to marry a beta. She can choose to say no," Elle says harshly. "No offense, but I'm not marrying any of you." She drops her voice low and nods toward us claimed. "And no way would I steal a man from one of you girls."

Violet scoffs. "She's right. I'm only marrying an alpha."

The curvy one, Marissa, folds her arms over her chest and studies the men with interest, but otherwise, she stays quiet. That seems to be her way, but I wonder how long she'll stay like that if she ends up liking one of these guys.

"Me too," the blonde one, Cecily, adds. "Ryne, if you're interested, let's chat. Otherwise, why bother?"

I have to bite my tongue at that comment.

"I'm gonna be alpha someday," one of the new betas says. His muscles ripple under his shirt, and aside from Ryne, he's probably the most handsome man I've ever seen, with a strong jaw and devastating smile that he's throwing at Cecily.

She doesn't look impressed.

"So if one of the lunas gets picked by a beta, and one of us doesn't, that means we're heading to the mating house. Including me?" I cross my arms and challenge him. I need to know how serious this is.

"Including you. Good luck, Poppy." He turns to his betas. "While Poppy is my fated mate, I recognize the need to strengthen my pack. I'll be choosing one of the lunas. Poppy is a strong woman and would make a fine wife for any of you."

My mouth turns to ash. I can't believe what I'm hearing. "Where's Nico?" I ask, voice cracking. He's the only other one I'd consider, but considering our conversation the other day, I'm pretty sure he's already backed out. I suddenly wish he hadn't.

"I released him from his pledge. He deserves time to mourn losing Nova."

"Oh, so he's devastated to lose his mate, but you're just fine losing yours?"

"I'm an alpha," he snaps. "I do what's best for my pack at all times."

I grit my teeth and back down. I don't know what else to say. There's nothing left. But it looks like we're fighting a losing battle once again.

CHAPTER 10

I'M NOT GOING through with this harvest. No way am I marrying some random beta or getting stuck in a mating house. If I have to, I'll run for The Sanctuary. In the meantime, the Resistance still needs my help. They started using the poppy as a symbol of solidarity with each other, a simple way to know who's on their side, because I stood up for what is right in front of everyone. Who would I be if I backed down now? So I'll be quiet, and I'll pretend, but it won't last long.

"We've prepared a picnic brunch for you all to get to know each other," Madame Delphine says. I notice she doesn't have her usual enthusiasm, and I wonder if she's as angry with Ryne as I am. "Please, enjoy yourselves."

The August heat is already too much. I'm sweating and want to get out of the sun. Luckily, the tables are set up underneath the shade of the weeping willows, and I hurry to them, plopping myself down with folded arms, still glaring at Ryne. I have no interest in putting on a pretty smile and acting as if any of this is okay. Too much has changed for us. And it's not as if I'm going to marry another man anyway. The Carolina Pack can forget all about me.

I'll be long gone before they can touch me.

The lunas are quick to surround Ryne, except for Elle. She sits down next to me and whispers under her breath. "This is all a bunch of bullshit."

I let out a startled laugh. I don't know if I've ever heard Elle curse before, but I don't blame her. She's lost so much for this to be the outcome, almost as much as I have, and for what? For us to prance around for a bunch of entitled men to "pick" us like we're livestock? I'm so over this.

"Hi there." An attractive man sits down right next to me. "I'm Bellamy. And you are?"

It's not the gorgeous guy who claimed he would be an alpha one day. That guy is still busy trying to get the lunas' attention. But this man isn't easy to overlook either. He's got curly black hair and smooth dark skin, the greenest eyes I've ever seen, and a relaxed smile.

Bellamy . . . a nice name too.

I don't say anything because I assume he's talking to Elle, but when she doesn't answer and elbows me in the ribcage, I startle. "Uh, I'm Poppy, but you probably already know that."

"Oh, because everyone knows who you are, is that right?" he teases.

I don't know if this is supposed to be flirty, but I'm not buying it. "I'm your alpha's fated mate, and I was very publicly engaged to another beta before getting kidnapped. Of course you know who I am." These games we're all playing are ridiculous.

He chuckles low and raises a shiny glass of ice water to me before taking a long drink. I can't help but notice the way his throat bobs as he swallows. It's sexy, and I shoot Elle a "he's all yours" look because, really, they would look fantastic together, but she just winks.

"You're right," he says. "I do know who you are, but that doesn't mean I know you." His gaze holds mine, interest swirling behind those bright green eyes. "But I'd like to."

My cheeks flush, and Elle coughs. "I'm going to go mingle." Then she leaves me alone with this man I'm now certain is flirting with me.

"Why are you flirting with me?" I blurt out. He raises an amused eyebrow, and I backtrack. "I just mean, there are other women here, and lunas at that. Why would you single out a rejected mate?"

He sets his glass down and leans in so our noses are only an inch apart, swamping me with his distinct spicy scent. It's so male, but it's also so different from Ryne's woodsy musk that it's jarring. I never thought I'd be this close to another man again. "You're special, and just because Ryne's too blinded by his position as alpha to see it doesn't mean I don't."

"Sure." I roll my eyes, but I don't back down or lean

away. This is an intriguing game we're playing, and maybe Elle's right that this is all a stupid distraction, but at least, it's a distraction. I need that now more than ever.

"It's true. I've been at all the festivals and have watched you every time, kicking myself for not pursuing you when I had the chance." He catches a strand of my hair between his fingers and twirls it. "And I only signed up for this because I knew you were back."

My mouth pops open, and I inadvertently sigh. Why can't Ryne be like this? Bellamy is more forward than any man I've ever met. He knows exactly what he wants: me.

I'm still a little thrown by him and his forwardness. I'm of two minds, and I don't know which one will win today. The first is to tell him to go to hell and stick with my plan of helping as many girls as possible get to The Sanctuary, staying single in the process. It's not going to be easy, and I know that it means a life of hardship and heartache, but it's also a life spent helping others.

But the other part of me wonders what it would be like to just give in. To let this beautiful man love me. To not have to worry about Ryne and death and lycans. Of course, the fact that I am one is a problem.

I glance over at him and catch a flash of red on his lapel.

I reach out and run my fingers over the soft petals. "You have a poppy." I wonder if he knows what it means or if he just has one because it shares my name.

He grins. "I do. Shauna gave it to me."

My eyes flash up to his. If Shauna gave it to him, that means he's in the Resistance.

"So you know . . ." I let my words trail off.

He glances up to where Ryne is chatting with Madame Delphine. A dark look shadows his face.

"I do. And it seems to me that Ryne is never going to be fully in even if he says he is."

"What's that supposed to mean?" But I'm pretty sure I already know. Ryne had me fooled too. Maybe he fooled the whole Resistance.

Bellamy shakes his head. "Not here. We'll talk about it on our date tomorrow night."

He's so sure of himself, but not in the arrogant way Ryne is.

"Date?" I ask.

He nods. "They're speeding up the process since we new betas have less than three months to make our choices. You'll have dates almost every night."

The other betas are leaving their tables, and Ryne walks away from Madame Delphine toward the house. Bellamy stands. "I guess it's time to go."

"I guess it is." I'm staring into his eyes, and I can't seem to look away. I'm so broken, and I doubt any man will be able to put me back together; I'm going to have to do it myself. But if someone wants to try, maybe I should let him.

He tears his gaze away and takes a step from the table. I reach out and grab his hand.

He glances down. "You okay?"

"Bellamy. If you're serious, tell Delphine that all my dates are with you."

His worried face splits into a wide smile, and a dimple appears on his left cheek. "I wouldn't have it any other way."

Then he squeezes my hand once more and strides across the lawn. I watch his retreating back for a moment, unsure of what I've just done. Then I glance up at the house. Ryne stands on the balcony, staring at me, a storm of torment brewing in his eyes. I recognize that possessive expression. I've seen it time and again when we're together. But I'm tired of the false hope, of the games and broken promises, so this time when our gazes meet, I'm the first to look away.

CHAPTER 11

"YOU'RE REALLY GOING to date Bellamy?" Elle lies on my bed, watching me and Faye dress and get ready for our dates. I nod and thumb through my dresses. I have no idea what to expect tonight, so I'm not sure what to wear.

"You're an idiot," Faye says. "But at least you'll make Ryne jealous."

"She's not wrong," Elle adds.

"What am I supposed to do? Wait around for Ryne to decide I'm worthy again? It's stupid. He's made it clear how he feels about me, and I'm not exactly on board with his 'let's keep things the same' agenda."

"Did you forget what you are? You can't date a wolf," Faye says.

"Didn't stop Ryne from declaring I would," I snap.

"She shouldn't be dating anyone." Elle sits up. "A little harmless flirting is one thing, but dating someone else puts your relationship at risk. Do you have any idea how lucky you are to be fated? I would kill for that."

"It obviously doesn't mean anything." I pick out a dress that Joanna had modified for me. It's fitted in the bodice with a flowy, feminine skirt, and it makes me miss her in the worst way.

"But it does. Ryne's acting like a fool now, but he will come around. And it's not fair of you to string Bellamy along because you and I both know that, if Ryne were to come back to you now, apologize, and get rid of the mating houses, you'd jump right back into his arms."

I think about her words for a moment, wondering if they're true. I don't know. I don't want to admit that she's probably right. Because wouldn't that make me weak?

"But he's not going to do that, so why should I wait around?"

Faye shakes her head. "Y'all are focusing on the wrong thing. What are you going to do come the full moon?"

"Madame Delphine will think of something—she always does." Besides, it doesn't seem that complicated to me. Just sneak me off to be somewhere by myself and lock me in. I have enough control over my lycan that it's not as if I'll be howling and drawing attention, and I won't leave to go off and bite people either. It won't be the most fun night, but it wouldn't be any worse than sleeping in that dark basement, fearing for my life.

Except even as I think about that sensible plan, I

know what I really want to do. I want to run away from Drayton Hall so I can hunt down Laik and his cronies. I'd do anything to take those evil lycans out. They need to be stopped, and I'm pretty fearsome in my own lycan form, but then again, so are they. And there are far more of them than there are of me.

"And is she going to think of something for the rest of your life? If you hook up with Bellamy, this won't be just for this month."

"If things get that far." Which, to be honest, they probably won't. Once Bellamy sees how broken I am, he's sure to bail on me for one of the better options. "But I'm not going to worry about that yet. I've got too many other things on my mind."

"Whatever. Just don't say we didn't warn you. What do you think we'll be doing tonight?" Faye changes the subject. "Justin and I haven't been out in ages. I hope we get to go off alone, no offense."

I don't know what to expect for my first date with Bellamy. Maybe it'll be a dinner out, dancing, or even a stroll along the riverside. Whatever it is, I hope Faye is wrong and we're not sent off alone with the men. Bellamy seems okay, but I don't know him—I can't trust the men I do know, let alone someone new.

We all gather in the hallway, but the betas are nowhere in sight. Elle hangs back. She's no longer dressed like a house mother but is instead wearing one of the boring black day dresses we claimed girls have to wear sometimes. She insisted she's not dating anyone, but I have a feeling she's not going to get a choice in the matter.

Madame Delphine looks her over. "You have a date tonight."

Elle glowers at her. "I told you I'm not going."

"Please, don't make this harder than it already is—for all of us."

Elle crosses her arms. "I'm a luna, so I don't have to date them if I don't want to." Madame Delphine opens her mouth to argue, but Elle rushes on. "But in the interest of not making your life more difficult, I'll agree to date Ryne, Justin, or Bellamy. Just not Dante or Lev."

Dante is the handsome wolf who boasted that he's going to become an alpha, and Lev isn't much better. They're clearly here to land a luna, which is exactly why Elle wants to keep them at arm's length.

Madame Delphine rubs her eyes. "I can work with that. You still need to put something else on, though. Tonight is a group date."

Faye groans, and I chuckle.

Elle comes back downstairs in a plain white dress. I'm sure she thought it would make it look like she didn't care about the date, but she still looks gorgeous. The color makes her inky skin pop and her braided hair stand out.

Three cars are waiting for us, and I manage to snag one with Faye, Delphine, and Elle, thank goodness. None of us say much on the drive over, though, because the driver isn't someone we know. Well, Delphine probably does know him, and we take our cues from her and keep our mouths shut.

In no time at all, we slide from the cars, decked out in gorgeous dresses as usual, and are met with a row of handsome smiles. I zero in on Bellamy because I can't bear to look at Ryne and his date, Violet. She's been all over him the second she laid eyes on him, and even more so since he declared he's looking to marry a luna, so apparently she doesn't care about fated mates any more than he does.

They're a match made in my own personal hell, and I refuse to watch their courtship unfold.

"Do you like popcorn?" Bellamy cuts into my thoughts.

"I love it, actually." Mostly because it reminds me of home and so many better memories than the ones I've made in this city, but he doesn't have to know that. It was the one snack we could have as often as we wanted at home because we were never short on corn. I can still remember the sound of the kernels popping on the hot stove and the anticipation of the salt coating my tongue.

"And what about movies?" he adds. "Any favorite movies I should know about?"

I blink at him in disbelief. I've heard about movies—we all have—but I didn't know they still existed. "I've never seen one."

Bellamy raises his dark eyebrows and smirks, making my stomach swoop a little. "Just you wait."

We're ushered inside the building and taken to a

huge room with row after row of padded seats facing a vast white wall that almost looks like it could be a window if it wasn't so opaque. I settle in next to Bellamy, and he slings his arm around the back of my chair, tugging me into his warmth.

A couple of middle-aged claimed women come around to distribute bowls of salty popcorn and tall cups of water to each couple. I hardly notice as the couples spread out because I'm too distracted by Ryne and his date. In spite of not wanting to see them, I can't keep my eyes off the pair. They're several rows ahead of us and talking to each other in low voices, their faces close. When Violet runs her fingers along his neck, I see red and clutch the armrest.

"You want to know something about me?" Bellamy's whisper is hot against my ear, and a shiver zaps down my spine. "I love a good challenge."

That snaps me out of it. I turn to glower at him, taking in his wild green eyes and the flirtation in his smile. "I don't think you realize how much of a challenge it's going to be to come between fated mates," I confess. This is not fair to him at all. "Even if we're broken up."

He leans back, relaxing, and gives me a wink. "I'm not worried, Poppy. By the Harvest Moon Festival, Ryne will be a distant memory, and I'll be the one you look for in a crowded room."

"Oh, you really think so?" Maybe I'm flirting a little too.

Maybe I like it. Maybe I need something to keep my

mind off the budding romance between Ryne and Violet by having one of my own.

"Oh, I know so."

The lights dim, and before I process everything going on between us, the screen lights up. I gasp, stunned by all that brightness seemingly coming from nowhere. It flickers to a scene of people larger than life, humans from a distant place and time, long before the world was lost to the shifters and lycans. As the movie starts, a miracle unfolds: I forget all about Bellamy *and* Ryne.

CHAPTER 12

I MAY GET LOST in the movie, but I don't stay there. After the novelty wears off, my eyes roam to the back of Ryne's head. He's got his arm tight around Violet's shoulders, and my stomach sours.

Bellamy's hand finds my chin, and he slowly turns my face so I'm looking at him. There's concern in his eyes, but he doesn't acknowledge Ryne at all. "Do you trust me?" he whispers through the dark.

"No," I admit. "I don't trust any men these days."

"Fair enough. Who is your closest friend in the house?"

"Elle."

I crane my head around, looking for her, and then chuckle when I find her sitting with Justin and Faye. She's two seats away from them, shoveling popcorn in her mouth. They are making out. I have no idea where her date went, but she probably already scared him off.

The woman is not interested in dating, let alone marriage. And although Madame Delphine made it seem like Elle would be getting her way tonight, she still ended up sitting next to Lev until he disappeared.

Bellamy follows my eyes. "Okay. Well then, would you be okay taking a walk with me as long as we bring Elle along?"

"Sure."

Despite the interesting movie, I want to get away from Violet and Ryne.

We leave the theater after getting permission from Madame Delphine. Bellamy holds out his arms, so Elle and I both tuck our hands in the crook of his elbows. Elle looks at me and winks. She seems more than happy to get away from Faye and Justin.

"And where'd your date go?" I tease her.

She shrugs. "He went home after I told him I'd kill him if he so much as breathed on me."

Everyone laughs, and I turn to Bellamy. "Where are we going?" I ask.

"The best-kept secret in town. My house."

I balk for a second. I don't want to go to his house, even with Elle around.

"Don't worry. It's not what you think. There are many people at my house that I want you to meet. I probably have more claimed servants than any other beta."

I snort. "If you think that's gonna make me like you more, then you have no idea who I am."

"But I do know who you are, and I can guarantee this is going to make you like me more."

Elle helps me out. "You know. You're a little too confident for your own good. Poppy's heart really isn't for the taking."

His eyes sparkle. "Fine. I'm willing to put my money where my mouth is, so to speak."

"Go on," Elle says.

"If by the end of the evening I have impressed Poppy, then I get a kiss from her."

"And if you don't?" I ask, my cheeks already burning at the thought of kissing him.

"Then I get a kiss from Elle."

Elle gasps and shoves him away, and he laughs. I stumble a little, and he catches me, his eyes sparkling. Either way, he ends the night with a kiss. The man is smarter than I thought and an even bigger flirt than Faye.

"I'll go for that," I say, actually liking the idea of Elle having a guy to distract her from her grief. "What about you, Elle? Will you take his wager?"

She stares at me for a long time, sadness in her eyes, and then she nods, and her face splits into a fake grin. "Guess I'll be getting a kiss tonight, so I probably should get to know you a little more." She takes his other arm once again and then begins to pepper him with questions about his past.

He tells us that he grew up in the pack houses and fought his way to beta. He's been a beta warrior for ten years and planned for many more before he took an interest in me. That part makes me blush even more, and I ignore Elle's raised eyebrows.

The walk doesn't take long, and soon we are standing in front of a huge southern mansion. It's almost as big as Ryne's place, which must mean Bellamy is a well-respected beta within the pack.

He pushes the oak front door open, and I walk inside, followed by Elle.

The entrance hall is wide with large rooms on both sides. Each is furnished with squashy couches and chairs. And there are women everywhere.

Some are asleep under blankets; others are chatting in low voices. A few have books in their hands.

A few more are sprawled out on the floor, playing board games.

Elle looks at me with her brow furrowed. "I don't understand what I'm looking at."

"Me neither," I admit.

Bellamy leans forward, keeping his voice low. "I'm not a fan of the mating houses. My mother once lived in them, was raped by wolves on a nightly basis. Obviously, I never knew her, but these women are living reminders of who she was. Betas sometimes take women home for a week or two if both parties agree. So I do the same thing. I bring home two or three women at a time for a couple of weeks from several different mating houses in the city. But I don't sleep with them. I let them rest and relax. My staff of retired women feed them well and care for them. We have a formal dinner almost every night. Most nights, I have between thirty and forty girls here."

My mind immediately goes to Abi, and I wonder if she's found sanctuary here. I had no idea things like this existed in the city, and I'm completely overcome by it. Bellamy really is what he says he is—resistance. And a good man at that.

"Does Ryne know about this?" I ask.

"He does."

"And he's okay with it?"

The answer to that question might kill me, but I have to know the truth. I don't know why I'm looking for redemption for him, but I can't help it.

"He tolerates it. Now, come meet everyone over dessert."

Elle doesn't wait. She's quick to make her rounds, chatting with the other women as if they're all old friends, though I'm sure she's never met them. I'm a little more reserved while I search for Abi's face. I need to find her, to make sure she's okay. "Do you know what happened to Abi?" I ask as Bellamy pulls out a seat for me at his long dining table.

"Who?" He sits next to me at the head of the table, and women begin bringing out trays of decadent sweets. I grab one of the chocolate tarts and set it on my plate.

"She's new. She went to the mating house back in April."

His eyes spark. "Oh, the girl who distracted the

wolves long enough for Grady to run off with his mate. How could I forget? But I'm sorry. I haven't seen her."

My heart plummets, fear trickling through my body. What if she's dead? Thorn probably had her killed. It's something he would do—end her life for being defiant and forget all about her the next day. Just another girl who failed, another girl who died at his hands. My eyes start to water, and my stomach goes hollow. Somehow, I just know Abi isn't doing well and probably isn't even alive.

"Hey, don't worry. I'll find her for you, okay? And when I do, I'll bring her to the house, and you can come out for dinner to make sure she's doing alright."

I meet his eyes, searching for sincerity. I still don't know if I can really trust him, if there's another angle he's playing here. Maybe he's like that other beta, Dante, who joined the claiming, acting like he'd become an alpha someday. If Bellamy fought to get this position in the pack, who's to say he isn't trying to take Ryne out, using me as part of his plan?

"I know you don't trust me," he supplies as if reading my mind. "But you will. I promise."

Elle plops down in the seat on his other side, directly across from me, her smile bright and her tone joyful. It's the happiest I've seen her since her father was killed. "I have to hand it to you, Bellamy. You're the real deal. If Poppy won't give you a kiss at the end of the night, I will. Heck, I'll even slip you some tongue."

She's joking, right? I've never seen her be so forward

with a man. Ever. But then she bursts out laughing, and so do I, Bellamy's tanned face flushing scarlet.

"Elle and Bell, it has a nice ring to it," I tease.

She waves her hand and gives Bellamy a more serious expression. "Oh please, you should know that I never want to get married. Not to an alpha or a beta or anyone, for that matter. Don't waste your time trying with me because the only way I'm getting married is if someone drags me down the aisle."

"Practice dragging lunas down aisles," he jokes. "Got it."

She laughs at that. "And don't say I didn't warn you about Poppy. She's already spoken for."

His eyes go dark, still trained on her. "We'll see about that."

My chest burns. I'm not sure how to parcel out my feelings. He's doing everything I wish Ryne would. And he's treating me better too. But I thought Ryne was a good man as well, and there was a time when he was sweet to me, when he made me promises and treated me like I was his world. I don't know that I can trust my own judgment.

After dessert, Elle stays in the house with the other women, talking about her hopes for the future after the alpha king is in place. Apparently there are a lot more Resistance shifters out there than I originally thought, and more pop up every day. Several are planning to fight for the throne. She believes one will win, and even though she's heartbroken her father didn't succeed, she's hopeful for the future of the kingdom. To see her so open about it makes me nervous but gives me hope, too, like maybe it's going to actually happen. It can't come soon enough. We've got less than three months until the harvest festival, and I've still got to figure out what to do about the coming full moons.

"I want to show you something," Bellamy whispers, taking my hand and leading me back outside. I don't really want to leave Elle behind, but Bellamy has given me no reason not to trust him after tonight. We go through the front door and around to a little side yard bursting with roses. The house has low lights, casting the garden into a golden haze. The scene is beautiful and smells even better than it looks.

He leads me up to another garden bed, this one brimming with bright red poppies. He picks one and hands it to me. "I thought about you for months after I first saw you, wishing I'd entered the claiming so I could court you."

Twirling the flower between my fingers, I stare at it, not knowing what to say and scared of what I'll find in Bellamy's face if I look at him. I never expected something like this. For a man to be so open with me, to want me this much. Not even Knox was like this when we first started dating. And Ryne did everything he could to fight our bond, only truly giving in to fate when we were out in the wilds.

Bellamy continues. "These roses have been here for ages, but this is the first year I cared about the garden."

His thumb brushes under my chin and tilts my face up to his. "And the first year I planted poppies."

Worries of him using me to get to Ryne drift away on the summer breeze. My lips part as he leans forward, our faces mere inches apart. "Can I kiss you?" he asks softly. It's different than with Ryne, who aggressively takes what he wants. Ryne would kiss me without waiting for permission.

This isn't better. Not worse. Just different.

It's to be expected—the wound is still so fresh. My broken heart has nothing to do with the potential for Bellamy to make me happy. He could heal it in time. And if anyone can help me move on, surely it's someone as attentive and determined as this handsome man. I know it's not fair to him to be my second choice, but he obviously doesn't care. He wants me anyway, I'm his number one, and I deserve to be happy after everything I've been through.

At least, that's what I tell myself as I nod consent, and Bellamy's lips brush against mine. He's soft at first, tentative, until I open my mouth to him. A low groan rumbles through his core, and the kiss turns passionate and exploring, our tongues pulling and prodding, our lips bruising. He presses me up against the house, and though he's not Ryne, and it's not the same, my body still responds, and my thoughts still float away.

But my heart?

My heart is back there in that theater, being ripped to shreds.

CHAPTER 13

ELLE SITS across from me at breakfast the next day, her eyes sparkling. I didn't tell her about the kiss with Bellamy last night. She spent the car ride home prattling on about the different girls she met and things we could do to help them. I barely heard what she said. My mind was on Bellamy and Ryne.

It still is. I can't quite seem to wrap my head around the fact that Ryne has written me off completely. I could probably be happy with Bellamy. Logically, it makes sense, and my body responded to his touch, but my heart will always ache for what could've been. Can I really defy fate?

Elle doesn't say anything until everyone else sits down. Our little group is not one I would've imagined at the beginning of the year. Faye and Samantha have their heads pressed together, whispering about something. Joy sits next to me, and while she seems to be doing better now that Faye is back, she's still withdrawn and reluctant to engage. Raven sinks down next to Elle, looking defeated, and picks at her food.

The lunas all sit together on the other side of the room, the older girls taking care of the younger. Violet and Cecily seem to be the leaders of their little group, which makes sense since they are the oldest. They don't have any interest in mingling with us, almost acting as if we don't even exist. Marissa is unaffected by it all, and poor Elle is stuck in the middle, not that she seems to mind. Elle has always been the type to do whatever she wants.

"So, Poppy," Elle begins with a smirk. "I didn't get a kiss from Bellamy last night, so that means you must've."

"What?" Faye gasps, turning on me with a huge grin. "You kissed him?"

I glare at Elle. "Yes. I did." I don't want to talk about this. I still don't understand it myself.

"And?" Elle asks, practically bouncing in her seat.

I blush and stare at my food.

Joy nudges me, which is surprising because Joy has been quiet as a mouse since I returned from the wilds. "Come on, we all want to know."

If I don't tell them, they'll never stop asking. "It was nice. He's not Ryne, obviously, but he's sweet."

"Is he a good kisser?" Raven raises her eyebrows suggestively.

I nod, and the table erupts with laughter.

Faye drops her voice to a whisper. "Excuse me, little princess, but weren't you and Ryne sleeping together?"

My blush deepens, and a few of the nearby girls gasp.

"I don't see how that's relevant." I drop my eyes. That's the least of my worries, actually. It's the lycan problem that I don't think we'll be able to get past. I can't be with Bellamy—he would never want to marry a woman who could kill him once a month.

"We're supposed to be pure." Samantha narrows her eyes. "If you're not a virgin, you're supposed to be sent to a mating house."

My whole body goes cold at her words, and I want to throttle Faye for blabbing.

Elle waves a hand. "You were with Ryne though. It's different because he's the alpha, so he's the one that gives his blessing for the weddings. Honestly, I doubt most of the wolves care about purity."

All the girls stare at me, but I don't have anything to say. It took two of us to do what we did, and I don't see Ryne apologizing for it.

"Some of them care about purity. It's a double standard." Faye rolls her eyes.

"Faye, I'm pretty sure you have no room to talk," Elle points out.

Faye straightens in her chair. "Justin and I are going to be married, so it doesn't matter what we do in private."

"Poppy thought that too."

Faye glares at Elle. "What Justin and I do when we're alone is nobody's business."

"Wait a minute, you too? Seriously, am I the only one who follows the rules?" Samantha asks, and Raven giggles.

Elle wiggles her eyebrows. "Now, you guys understand how this works. Bellamy has all but proposed to Poppy, so that leaves you three to battle it out for Dante and Lev." Elle points her fork at Joy, Samantha, and Raven.

"They're going to go for the lunas." Raven sighs. "We don't stand a chance."

"But the lunas have no interest in the betas at all. Marissa is like me and doesn't want to get married. And Violet and Cecily are going after Ryne because he's the alpha." Elle's insistence is like a knife to the heart. What if Ryne wants one of them back?

"I don't want to get married either." Raven grips her fork. "I hate this whole system."

"Well, that certainly makes this easier." Elle winks. "Raven, we'll work on getting you out to The Sanctuary, and the same goes for anyone else who wishes to leave. But I'll have a conversation with Delphine about dates and make sure the ladies who stay get plenty of one-on-one time with Dante and Lev." A small smile creeps over Samantha's face, and it's sort of wonderful that we can talk about these things in the open like this.

I don't want to get their hopes up. "Maybe we

should be looking at getting all four of you to The Sanctuary. I'll go with you."

Even as I say the words, I'm not sure I mean them. I'd likely go and come crawling right back.

Elle grins at me. "And break poor Bellamy's heart? No way. But if the rest of you want to go, that can be arranged."

I don't know how she can be in such a good mood and talk about all this so nonchalantly. This is all so heavy, and I'm tired of it. I want Ryne to do what he said and make the mating houses and the claiming a thing of the past. He says that breeding can be done by paying women from the villages to come to the city, and I think he's probably right so long as they're treated with respect. It's not a perfect solution to the shifters' population problems, but it's certainly better than rape.

"Does going mean we'll never get to visit our village?" Joy speaks up, and we all turn to her. "It's not like I'm expecting to see my family again, but what if things change, and we can? I don't want to miss that opportunity. I'm not sure the panthers will be any better than the wolves, and if that's the case, then I'd rather stay closer to home."

We're all homesick, and her question makes my chest burn.

Elle offers a sad smile. "I don't have the answer to that, Joy. I'm sorry."

"I think I'll stay then." Joy shrugs, turning back to our food, and the rest of us exchange worried glances just as Madame Delphine enters the room, cutting off all conversation.

"Ladies, classes will resume after chores today. I expect my girls to show the lunas how we do things around here. Anyone sixteen and older will attend the same classes, and I'm bringing in another woman to teach the younger girls. There will be no more rankings as this is the last quarter and is highly unnecessary. As you know, the betas will be here each evening to take you out." She glances at her watch. "You have ten minutes until chores."

And just like that, life is *normal* again.

CHAPTER 14

THE NEXT FEW weeks pass in a blur. It's classes, chores, and dealing with obnoxious lunas during the days and romantic dates with Bellamy most nights. Sometimes we go out with other couples, but half the time we're alone. Elle joins us quite a bit. She still refuses to date Lev or Dante, so she only goes out with Bellamy or Ryne—just as she said she would. The girl is great at getting her way, and I kinda envy her for that.

Ryne rarely even looks at me. Though, one night, I didn't realize he was on the porch when Bellamy brought me home and gave me a long goodnight kiss. I found Ryne glaring at us before shifting into his wolf form and running away. I almost went after him, but my pride wouldn't let me. Why should I care? I'm the one who got dumped.

The whole thing is wearing on me.

A week before the full moon, I'm on the front porch,

waiting for Bellamy to arrive, wondering what on earth I'm going to do about us.

"You okay?" Bellamy asks as he approaches. We're well past small talk, but I'm still not sure if I'm ready to open up to him emotionally.

"Yeah, why?"

"You look sad." Those words hurt because they're true. I am sad.

I shrug it off. "I'm just worried about things, you know. There is still no alpha king, and I'm tired of trying to keep the Resistance a secret. I'm ready for change." And I want Ryne back, but I don't say that.

He grabs my hand. "I know. It seems like everything is in limbo, but it won't last forever. Besides, I have a surprise for you."

I give him a small grin. "You have a surprise for me almost every day."

"Yeah, but this is something I think you'll really enjoy." He takes my hand and leads me to his car. There's no driver tonight, and I ride in the front as we travel through the center of the city. I don't like this area. It's where most of the mating houses are located, reminding me of all the disappointments I've had since coming here. But I'm one of the lucky ones, right? This is such a horrible world we live in that I should consider myself lucky...

I expect him to park here, but when we keep going, my spirits lift. I was worried he was going to take me to see some of the women in the mating houses. It feels selfish that I didn't want to do that. We finally end up on the other side of the wolf city—on the outskirts, the opposite end of Drayton Hall. He pulls up to a beautiful estate with wolf shifters stationed all around it. It's got far more protection than even the claimed girls get. They nod to Bellamy as we drive up to the entrance.

"What is this place?" I ask.

But Bellamy stops the car and opens the door for me, and I get my answer. A group of four pregnant women strolls through a rose garden in the distance. They gaze over at us with lifted hands to shade the sunset's glare from their eyes, casting their faces in dark shadows. I imagine their expressions are filled with distrust at the sight of us. I'd never look at any man the same if I had to go through what they've gone through to end up here.

We should go.

It isn't right to come here on a date; it's like we're rubbing it in their faces that we're parading around on dates while they're here—not beta wives but baby makers all the same. If I ever have kids, I'll do anything to keep them with me. Being a beta wife would do that for me. Is pregnancy even possible now that I'm a lycan? Maybe I'm infertile, and I don't even know it yet. I want to say something to Bellamy, and my stomach churns at the thought of seeing what's inside this estate home, but I bite my tongue out of curiosity. It's good to know what the Resistance is dealing with, and I'd love to see if the pregnant mating-house women are treated as well as Ryne said they are.

"Unfortunately, we can't go inside." Bellamy seems to read my mind. "Well, you probably could, but this is the one place the women are allowed respite from the men. Only women inside unless they call on us for protection."

"Can't say I blame them," I mumble as we round the corner of the back of the house instead of heading inside.

A woman sits with her hands resting on her belly, though the belly in question is as flat as mine. Her hair hangs around her face, and when she looks up at us with that familiar blue gaze, my heart flutters.

"Abi," I gasp. I drop Bell's hand and race to my friend.

She rises from her chair and catches me in a hug. When I pull back, her eyes are round with disbelief. "I thought you were dead. I heard you got taken by lone wolves and assumed they had killed you. What are you doing here?" She stares at me like she's seen a ghost.

I shake my head. "I'm fine, but enough about me. How are you?" My voice cracks, and I wonder if I should've asked another question instead. Of course she's not doing well. She's been in a mating house for months, and now she's here, pregnant. I know that's the point, that eventually we're all going to have babies, or at least try, but to see it happen so fast is a shock.

"I'm okay." Her eyes dart to Bellamy.

I turn to mouth a big "thank you" to him.

"I'll be waiting in the car when you're ready to leave, but no rush. We've got all night."

I'm grateful for his thoughtfulness.

And then he's gone, and it's just me and Abi on this stupid huge porch, and everything comes flooding in at once. She must feel the same way because we fall into each other's arms, sobbing. I don't know how long we stay like that, but long enough for the tears to dry up into salty streaks down our cheeks. Then we sit on the porch swing, gently swaying, as we tell each other everything that's happened over the last four months.

Well, almost everything.

Abi can't handle explaining the details about the mating house, and I can't explain what it felt like to become a lycan and bite Knox the way I did. She's not happy about being pregnant because she doesn't want to contribute to the wolf city. She doesn't care that she gets better treatment away from the men for the next nine months. And I'm not happy about Ryne and everything he's put me through recently.

And when I tell her about Joanna, how she went with Grady to be with the horrible lycans that are biting humans, she becomes angry with shock. "I just can't believe they would do that," she keeps repeating. And I feel the same way, though I have a hard time blaming Joanna for anything. Grady demanded it, and she wasn't willing to leave her mate.

I take Abi's small hand in mine and squeeze. "If there's one thing I've learned this year, it's that people aren't always who they say they are."

"And sometimes people are exactly who they say

they are," she replies, her voice dark and filled with unknown horrors.

"Things are going to change," I whisper. "I'll get you out of here, and you can take your baby with you, or you can leave the baby with someone else to adopt, but I promise you're going to live in the panther sanctuary before you ever step foot in another mating house."

She scoffs and points to the men at the perimeter. "Do you see the security around here? I don't think I'm leaving until I have the baby, and as soon as I'm healed, it's back to the mating house for me."

"No." I'm adamant. "Don't think that. Trust me. I'll find a way. Between Madame Delphine and Elle and Bellamy, we can work it out. And if those bastards out there"—I point to the men on the perimeter—"won't let you out, I'll take it up with Ryne. He owes you that much for protecting us."

She nods, but I can tell she doesn't believe it's possible, and that only makes me more determined to keep my promise.

On the way home, my thoughts are all over the place, and I stare out the window, unable to say a word.

Bellamy holds my hand and gives it a squeeze. "You okay in there? I thought for sure seeing Abi would make you happy."

I give him a smile, a genuine one that I seem to only reserve for him these days. "I am so grateful for what you did, but seeing Abi was hard," I confess. "She's been through a lot, and now she's going to have to give up her baby. It's just one more reminder that this isn't right."

He goes still, his jaw ticking. "I wish there was more we could do." He's quiet for a long, drawn-out moment, which is rare for him. One of the things I enjoy about Bellamy is his constant chatter. He keeps matters light and my mind off of heavier things.

"I want to talk to you about something."

"Sure."

He hesitates again, and now I'm worried. "We've been at this for a month now and only have two left. How . . . how are you feeling about us? I mean, me, specifically. And please be honest. Don't just tell me what you think I want to hear."

My heart clenches. I owe him the truth, even if that means possibly losing him. "I'm not sure. I mean, you're probably the most genuinely good man I've ever met, and I care for you deeply. I enjoy our time together, I'm physically attracted to you, and I desperately want to love you, but I worry the fated mate bond between me and Ryne makes that impossible. I think I will always long for him even if I hate him too." I can't look at Bellamy while I speak. "I'm yours if you're willing to accept only part of my soul. If you're willing to understand that I'll never love you the way you love me but that I'll love you as much as I'm able and give you everything I can give."

The words tumble out, and I can feel the silent tears falling down my cheeks. Ryne has robbed me of this as well. The ability to love fully. The chance to be enough for someone as wonderful as Bell.

"What if Ryne were dead?" His voice goes dark.

I gasp and turn on him. "Are you planning on killing him?"

He backpedals. "No, no, no. Nothing like that. I was just wondering if that would change your feelings."

I stare at him for a long moment, afraid of saying the wrong thing. "I honestly don't know."

"But is it easier when he's not around?"

"Yeah. It is," I confess. "But if he were to die because of me, I'd break for good."

Bellamy nods. "Okay then. Don't worry. We're not killing Ryne." He worries that full bottom lip between his teeth, and I wonder where he's going with this. "I've heard of a pack out west where things are different. They're so far removed from this side of the kingdom that they barely even recognize the alpha king. They don't have mating houses, and they live openly with the humans. Once this is over, and we're married, I'm sure Ryne will release me from the Carolina Pack. And we can head out west, and you'll never have to see him again. Poppy, any part of your soul is worth more than you know. I'm willing to accept whatever you have to give."

My eyes water, and I can't think of what I've done to possibly deserve such a kind man in my life. "I think I would like that. But do you think maybe we can go find my family and bring them along as well?"

"We can bring whoever you want. Well, except Ryne."

I smile and squeeze his hand once again. It's hard to think about what comes after marrying Bellamy, but for the first time in a long time, I have hope that maybe my life won't always be horrible.

And then I see the waxing moon rising over the horizon, and I remember—I can never be with Bellamy, because I'm a lycan.

CHAPTER 15

THE NEXT MORNING, Madame Delphine calls me into her office.

"How are things going with Bellamy?" Her mouth is pressed in a straight line. She doesn't really approve of me dating him when I'm already fated to her son, but there is nothing I can do about that. Ryne's the one being an idiot. Not me.

"He's very good to me."

"Do you kiss him?"

I frown. "Yes." But I don't elaborate.

Madame Delphine sinks down into her chair. "I was afraid of that. How long before and after the full moon does your venom take them out?"

I swallow. I don't like thinking about my lycan form. "Three days."

"Okay. Then we need to get you out of town for a

week. I'll need a couple of days to organize things, but you'll take Raven to The Sanctuary."

"What about Joy and Samantha?"

"They haven't agreed to leave yet, but we'll see if I can change their minds. Either way, you'll stay there through the full moon and come back three days later. We won't tell Bellamy until after you've left because, if we tell him before, he'll insist on going with you."

"Okay."

It's the best solution. I hate deceiving Bellamy, and I dread the day I have to tell him what I am. That will likely be the end of us, and I'll be alone again.

THREE DAYS before the full moon, Elle takes me, Raven, and four of the mating-house women to the panther sanctuary. It's an all-day journey. The others find it grueling, especially when we have to don the heavy protective gear required for humans to cross the contamination zone, but it's no trouble for me. I put it on myself because I don't need the other women questioning what I am, but my lycan-self is growing stronger with the coming moon, and carrying gear is no issue. In fact, I suspect I may be getting stronger with each moon that passes, which makes sense considering what I've learned about lycans. I have increased stamina, my senses are clearer than ever, and I still have three days until the next renewal. It feels incredible, and I would consider myself lucky if I weren't in such a dangerous position. I'm hunted, and if anyone else finds out what I am, I could be killed. Elle is the only one in our group of seven who knows the truth, but she doesn't comment on it, and I'm not willing to reveal my secret to the others.

"This is where I'll leave you," Elle says, parking the jeep a half mile from the perimeter of the panther territory. "We've already sent word that you're coming. They're expecting all of you."

"But Derek is on our side," I argue, sliding from the passenger seat and helping the other ladies remove their protective gear. "You should come with us and see what it's like in Savannah. It's so much better than what the wolves have created in your kingdom. The panthers have the freedom to live how they want, they mix species without prejudice, and people share enough that nobody is in poverty."

The other women stare at me with dazed expressions. I get it. I would hardly believe it myself if I hadn't seen it with my own eyes.

"It's really that good, huh?" Elle asks skeptically.

"It's wonderful. We could have something like that in our pack if Ryne would pull his head out of his ass and take control the way he promised he would."

Raven snorts. "I was wondering when you were going to stop being so forgiving of that man. Not that it matters. We're never going back there, and I hope to never see his disgustingly handsome face again."

My stomach clenches at the thought of never seeing

him again, and I shake my head. "You already know I'm going back. I'm only here to make sure you guys are set up and have everything you need."

"You really want to go back to the wolves?" Raven asks. "After everything you've been through?"

"Yes, I really do."

The women stare at me like I've grown a second head. "But why?" Raven presses. "We're here now and get to start a new life. Do you know how lucky that is? Chances like these don't come around often."

They barely come around at all, but my mind is made up. "This isn't where I'm meant to be," is all I say. But what I'm thinking is that I can't bear to leave Ryne or Bellamy. Not so suddenly. Maybe one day, I'll come back here to live with the panthers or go out west with Bell if he'll be willing to marry a lycan, but that day is not today. Besides, I still need to see things through with the mating houses, and I want to reunite with my family. I have too many responsibilities, too much hanging in the balance, to leave right now.

"You really think you're meant to stay in that pack?" one of the mating-house women says, frowning deeply. "You won't be thinking that when you end up where I did."

"If I left now, I'd always wonder."

Her eyes narrow. "Wonder what? How many babies you wouldn't get to raise? How many men would get to have your body?"

"Wonder if I could've fixed things," I reply, agitated.

"That's my goal. I want to end the mating houses altogether, and I can't do that if I leave. I'm not going back to get a mate. I'm going back to help more of you."

Elle nods because she gets it, but the rest shake their heads.

"Sure looks like you're going back for Ryne." Raven frowns. "Whatever. Your loss. Let's go." And with that, the girl turns on her heels and stomps in the direction of the panthers.

She doesn't look back.

I say a quick goodbye to Elle. She promises to see me in seven days then returns to the jeep and drives off, the dust from her tires kicking into the air.

Seven days . . .

No way I'm sitting around here for seven critical days. Ryne is about to go through some kind of wolf-lycan hybrid renewal, Laik's pack is probably planning to bite more humans against their will, and what's left of my family is back home in their village, oblivious to the danger they're in. I won't stand for it. What kind of person would I be if I stayed here?

That's the question that spurs me on the day of the full moon, and after making sure the women are settled and happy in The Sanctuary, I leave the city, hours before sundown. I'm on foot, but I don't have to worry about the radiation zone, and I'm fast. When the moon rises, I shift into my lycan as easily as breathing.

And then I'm even faster—impossibly fast.

The forest comes alive under my heightened senses,

my claws slicing through any branches that get in my way, my mind clearing, my ears attuned to every small sound. It only takes an hour to get to my village. When I finally see it after all this time, I want to cry, and if I could, I absolutely would.

I spot the white church and the little schoolhouse and the huge tree that I often climbed with Willow . . . And there, in the middle of the town square, stand the other lycans.

My stomach hardens at the sight of them. Somehow, deep in my gut, I knew they'd come here tonight. I hate that I was right. There aren't many of them. Only three. But three is already too many.

And there isn't a wolf shifter in sight.

At least, Laik isn't here with dozens of lycan—I can handle three.

I hope . . .

I do a quick glance around and listen intently, but the people are all tucked into their homes. I watch the lycans and wonder if they can sense me. Maybe they don't even register it. They seem to be conferring about something, and if I wanted to, I could listen in on the conversation, but I deliberately keep myself out of it so they can't sense me.

Then they split up, all heading for different houses. A large male heads for my old house, the little one next to the big tree, and I don't even think. I sprint out in the open and leap up on him. There is no way I'm letting him get my family.

He bucks under my grip, but I've taken him by surprise. Without thinking, I bite down on the back of his neck, his sinewy flesh tearing in my jaws. He howls and throws me off. I go flying and land in the dirt, pain snapping at my right shoulder, but I'm up in two seconds flat, shaking the stars out of my eyes.

My plan worked though. He's heading straight for me, blood pouring down his back, my family forgotten.

Who are you? The lycan stands over me, breathing heavily. I can't believe that after I attacked him, he still wants to talk, but I'm not playing that game.

I lunge for him again, this time using my claws to slice open his stomach. He howls and drops to the ground, his eyes pleading with mine.

Why are you doing this? he demands

I'll not let you hurt the people in this village, I reply.

Hurt them? I'm protecting them from the wolf shifters.

The fact that he thinks that is ludicrous. *By turning them? That's hardly protection.*

The lycan shakes his head. *We don't turn them.*

The wheels spin in my head. I wonder if the man is telling the truth or if he is just deceived by what's really going on. I know, for a fact, that humans are being bitten against their will. I also know not every human will survive the virus. And if they do, they'll still have lost their families and the lives they once knew.

What do you do with them after you kidnap them? I challenge.

Laik disperses them to safe houses.

Laik does no such thing. You're a fool for believing him. He puts them in camps and turns them all into lycan. Now get out of here, or I will kill you.

The lycan slowly rises to his feet and trudges from the village, but I have half a mind to go after him for being so foolish to begin with. I glance around for the other two lycans, but they're nowhere to be found. I'm sure they took people back with them, but there are too many possibilities for where they could have gone.

So Laik is smart enough to wait to bite the humans. He's got his pack out here doing his dirty work. I wonder how many actually know what's going on and how many are blind to the truth.

I stop under the tree by my own house, wondering if they are all hiding in the back corner, my dad ready to fight to protect his wife and son. Is Evan crying, or did he sleep through the whole thing? Is Mama praying with her eyes closed right now, or is she right there with Papa, ready to fight to the death? If I went through that door right now, they'd attack me. I have no doubt they wouldn't even hesitate to kill me—the evil lycan.

My blood boils, and anger scorches me from the inside out. Anger at Laik for what he's doing. At myself for not being able to see my family again. And also at Ryne. Especially at Ryne. I can't believe he didn't have wolves protecting the villages after last month. He made such a fuss about it, and yet I'm the only one here—another lycan, something they'd kill if they saw me. I don't know what Ryne is doing, but it's nothing good, that's for sure.

After doing one more sweep of the village just to make sure no lycans are left, I turn and head back for the wolf city. Just as I'm crossing the taxing field, memories I can't seem to forget drown me in grief. It's like I'm right back there again, right back to the day Anders killed Willow for no good reason, and I was taken in her place. So much has happened that it feels like a lifetime ago, but right now I'm reliving it like it's happening all over again. I can still smell her coppery blood in the air, hear myself scream, and feel the rawness of it tearing my throat. I can see the horrified expressions branded on the onlookers' faces and the way my mother immediately handed me over to my sister's killer to protect herself.

I'd give anything to go back and redo that moment. Maybe I could coach Willow on how to act. Maybe I could say something right as we parted that would change the way she responded when Anders groped her. And yet, deep down, an honest part of me knows that Willow wouldn't have survived the claiming for long. She was always too proud, too headstrong, and fiercely independent. She reminds me so much of Joanna, but without a fated mate to protect her. If Grady hadn't stepped in for Joanna when he did, she'd have been lost the same way as my sister.

Anger racks me, and I want to howl and release my pent-up emotions into the night, but I hold them in because it would scare the villagers. Maybe the moon could sort my feelings out for me because, no matter how much time passes, I can't seem to do it myself. And maybe I never will.

Something hits me hard in the back, trying to push me to the ground, hard and so fast. I turn on my haunches, that horrible howl echoing from my lungs despite myself. Instinct takes over, and I ready myself for an attack. If it's another lycan, they're dead. If it's a wolf, I'll try not to kill them, but I'll do what I must. And if it's a human, I'll run to protect them.

"Don't do it," the woman yells in my face.

Not just any woman—Joanna stares up at me, a long knife in her hand and a fearsome glare in her warrior eyes.

"I've changed my mind," she goes on. "We can't take the humans to Laik. They're innocent, and he's no good."

I step back, realization taking hold. She thinks I'm one of the lycan working for Laik. I don't know what their plan was for tonight, but obviously it had something to do with taking humans to help build Laik's army. I want to tell her it's me, not the other lycan she came with, and that I'm here to help the humans. I want to beg her to come back with me to the manor so that we can hide her or take her to The Sanctuary even though I know she won't go anywhere without Grady. But most of all, I'd give anything to hug her. Just hug her.

But we can't communicate, and she has no idea who I really am.

"I mean it." She shakes her knife at me. "I'll kill you if I have to."

I step forward slowly, hoping she'll recognize the gesture as one of peace, but she spooks and takes off running, clumps of dirt kicking up behind her. Instinct tells me to make chase, but when I catch a glimpse of Grady's three-legged wolf on the edge of the woods, waiting for her, his eyes glowing in the darkness, I think better of it. I don't want anyone to get hurt, and Grady will engage me in a fight.

My heart drops, desperate for her to know who I am. But I can't risk trying, and the moon will be in the sky for several more hours at least. I'm stuck in this form.

I'm stuck.

So I let them go and head back toward the wolf city in search of Ryne, and when I find a band of young wolf shifters with their throats cut a mile outside of my village, I get the answer to my earlier question. Ryne *did* send wolves out here to protect these humans, but the lycans must have killed them. How many more wolves were killed tonight? And how many humans were taken?

No doubt, this was a coordinated attack, and Laik is planning something big.

CHAPTER 16

I'M careful to keep myself hidden once I get to the city. If a wolf shifter spots me, I'm in serious trouble, and while I could wait until sunup, this night is too important. I'll get to Ryne's house and just wait outside until I shift back, but hopefully I can catch a glimpse of whatever is going on with him.

Because, surely, something has happened. He didn't survive my bite for nothing.

I manage to keep to the alleys, and I spot the park by Ryne's house with its many trees. Great hiding spots for me. I edge my way there, keeping to the shadows, slow and methodical. Someone yells, and I narrow my vision at a group of wolves that have gathered in the middle of the park. I know what this is about, and I nearly roll my eyes. They should be out there protecting the villages, worried about the lycans, fighting for the humans, for their own brothers—instead, they are here, fighting

Ryne for his title of alpha. Did they wait until the full moon when they knew he'd be distracted?

It's a clever tactic, but as angry as I am with Ryne, I hope it doesn't work. I know where things stand with Ryne. A new alpha would be too unpredictable. I creep close enough to hear everything and scale a tree until I have a clear view of the wolves surrounding Ryne. He's covered in scratches and bite marks and blood. How many wolves have challenged him so far? How many does he have to kill or banish before they give up and accept he's too strong?

He shifts back into his human form and prowls in front of the group, naked and menacing. The fact that he can still shift like normal is good news—the best news, actually. He'd hate me forever if he lost his wolf-self to his lycan, and I watch him, completely unable to look away. He's beautiful like this, with the moon lighting him up like a beacon. He's radiant and terrifying, and he'll never be mine.

"Who challenges me now?" he roars. "I have been merciful so far, simply banishing the three wolves who fought me instead of killing them. But I'm done. If anyone else thinks they can beat me, it will be a fight to the death."

I wonder if Bellamy is in the crowd of wolves or out protecting a village somewhere. If he could see me now, would he still want me? I snort. Highly unlikely.

A large man steps forward, and recognition hits me. It's Dante, the handsome beta who claimed he would be an alpha someday. I wonder if he's taking the chance now that he's got lunas he's after. "Someone needs to fix your mistakes," he snarls. "It might as well be me."

"Dante. Are you sure about this?" Ryne sounds hurt. Betrayed. I would be too.

"It's time for a new alpha." Dante's voice echoes through the night, and then he shifts into a huge brown wolf. Ryne wastes no time shifting and lunging for him. I've seen Ryne fight before, but I've never seen him move so ruthlessly. His claws are out, shining like sharpened knives, and he's fighting like a madman. Within seconds, Dante's wolf is flat on his back, snarling and snapping his jaw. Ryne jerks Dante's neck around and bites him on the flank. The brown wolf immediately goes limp.

Ryne shifts back into his human form, and even from this distance, I can see the shock in his eyes. He wipes blood from his mouth. The wolf doesn't move.

Dante's dead.

"Anyone else?" Ryne snarls, and the whole crowd disperses, leaving Ryne alone with the dead wolf. Ryne limps in the direction of his house, and I stay in the tree, watching him go. He glances back at the dead wolf every once in a while, confusion and pain evident on his face. He may not understand what just happened, but I do.

His bite *alone* killed Dante.

He's part lycan now, and just like us, he can end wolf shifters with a single full-moon bite.

I drop back to the ground and keep to the shadows,

following Ryne. I manage to make it to his gate, without being seen, just as he's climbing his porch steps.

Can you hear me? I ask through the lycan-communication link.

I hold my breath and wait. If he can hear me, then my theory is correct, and he really is part lycanthrope. He spins around, anger warring on his face.

"Get out of my head," he shouts. His eyes search his yard, but he doesn't move, and I'm hidden behind a bush.

But you can hear me. How interesting. You know what this means, don't you?

"Get out of my head, or I will find you and kill you."

You would kill your fated mate? I thought that wasn't allowed.

"Poppy?" His voice softens. I peek out around the edge of the bush. He's sunk onto the steps, and his head hangs low.

I want nothing more than to comfort him, but that's not possible in this form. I glance up at the sky. The sun will be rising soon, and the moon will no longer have her hold on me. Thankfully it's the middle of the summer instead of the winter, or I'd be out here for several more hours.

Yeah, it's me. I'll come see you when the sun rises.

He stands, and for a second, I'm scared he's going to come after me, but instead, he turns around and slumps inside, leaving the door cracked open. It's the first time since he found out what I did to him that he's shown any indication that he wants anything to do with me. Not that I'd go running back into his arms.

There's too much bad blood there, but he does need to accept what happened tonight.

The sun is up about thirty minutes later, and I find myself back in my own body. I'm as naked as the day I was born, but it's nothing Ryne hasn't seen before.

I rush up to the front door, push it open, and close it quickly behind me.

"Poppy?"

I spin, but instead of finding Ryne, it's Callum who is waiting for me. He's got pants on and nothing else, and even from here I can smell the lycan on him. I wonder where he stayed last night, assuming he must have been locked in this house somewhere. He's lucky to have made it through the night. He quickly averts his eyes, but my nakedness is honestly nothing he hasn't seen either, considering how many times he's tended to my wounds.

"Let me get you some clothes." He disappears, and I stand awkwardly in the foyer. I wonder if it's just Callum and Ryne here or if there are others. I hope Ryne doesn't have a girl in his bed. That would be the worst. Would Ryne do that to me? Surely not, but I don't even know anymore. Ryne isn't who I thought he was.

Callum returns with a long shirt. "I can't find any shorts that will fit you."

"This'll work."

The shirt hits me mid-thigh, so I'll be careful when I

sit down, but for now, it covers everything. It's a button-down collared shirt, and it takes me a minute to button it all up. I roll up the sleeves so they don't hang down over my hands. The shirt smells like Ryne, and my stomach churns. I miss him so much—but I'm also so damn angry. It's a horrible feeling.

I follow Callum into the living room and find Ryne there alone. He glances up at me and gives me a once over in his shirt. I worry about what he might think, but his lips curl into a small smile, and he drops his eyes. Callum leans over and whispers in my ear. "That's the first time I've seen him smile in a month."

I don't respond and sink down onto the opposite side of the couch from Ryne, careful to keep myself covered up. I need to shower and get the lycan stench off me, need better clothes, need a lot of things, actually, but first, I must have this conversation.

"I told Callum what happened," Ryne says, not looking at me. Something about that stings, even though it shouldn't. He let Callum in, a boy he hardly knows, and he pushed me out like I'm the stranger.

"Including that we can talk telepathically and that you killed a wolf with a single bite?"

Ryne nods, his long hair hiding his face from me. I imagine that if I could see his eyes, they'd be even more haunted than my own.

"What do you think?" I turn to Callum.

Callum leans back in his own chair and rubs his chin. "Honestly, I think Ryne is some kind of hybrid.

We've never seen this before," His voice grows excited. "But it's a good thing. It might mean he can lead both the shifters and the lycan."

Ryne winces at that, saying nothing more.

"But do the lycans have to follow him like the shifters do?" I ask, thinking over the implications of this. "Like, could he become an alpha for us too?" I imagine Ryne stepping in and bossing Laik and Wanda around, telling them to leave the humans and wolves alone.

"I'm not sure. It's something we'll have to test on the next moon. You'd be perfect for it."

"If the lycans in this area have to follow him, that would solve a lot of problems, but I kind of doubt we'd get so lucky. You know our pack bonds are nothing like the wolf shifters'. They're more about intimidation than anything else."

"Yeah, but can you imagine how good that would be?" Callum smiles.

I nod because it would be good, but probably too good to be true. We're not wolf shifters. We never will be. "You're right, but we need to have someone else test it. I'm not good for that."

"Why not?"

"Because I'm his fated mate." I shrug, hating those two words. They don't mean anything anymore, and yet they always will. "I think the rules are different for us."

"That's fine. I'll test it myself then." Callum shoves his hand through his hair, and I can tell he's thinking hard, that scientific brain of his categorizing everything he knows. "I wish these rules were written down somewhere. No one really understands how all of this works."

"You can write it down."

"I am, but there is so much that doesn't make sense."

He's right, and talking about it is getting us nowhere. "There are other problems as well. I was at my village last night."

Ryne's head pops up, and he glares at me. "I thought you were at The Sanctuary."

Oh, so now he speaks? I glare right back. "I obviously left. Since when do I stay where I'm told?" I ask, realizing that I have more Joanna in me than I thought.

His lips twitch. "Truth. I hope you found it well guarded. I was worried about the villages last night and sent out some of my best men. Which is how I ended up being challenged. The ones who don't listen well stayed behind and got it in their heads that I needed to be taken out. They were some of Anders's cronies that got left behind."

"No. I did not find them well-guarded. In fact, I found wolf shifters on the edge of my village with their throats slit. They never saw it coming. I'm surprised you didn't know, considering you're their alpha."

Ryne jumps up and lets out a stream of curses. "You're right, but I was distracted by the challenges to my title. Callum, call Justin and the other betas. We need to figure out exactly what happened last night."

Callum rushes from the room, and Ryne approaches me, kneeling and taking my hands in his. There's no lingering scent of lycan on him, as if his infection never happened. He's still the wolf shifter I met nearly a year ago. He's still Ryne. "Poppy, I'm so sorry for what I've done. When I get back, can we talk?"

His words are like being drenched in ice water. I jerk my hands from his and shake my head. "You hurt me, Ryne. Deeply. And then you threw your betas at me like it would all be okay."

"About the betas—"

I hold up my hand. "We're through, Ryne. I'm with Bellamy now."

I don't know if I mean the words or not, but he cannot just expect me to be okay with him now that he's realized he's not going to shift into a monster. I don't wait for him to respond. I push him back and stand, heading in the direction that Callum went. I trust Callum to help me find a shower and women's clothing, and then I'm going back to the manor and getting on with my life.

CHAPTER 17

I DON'T TALK to Ryne in the weeks that follow. For three days, I avoided Bellamy, and then I let him right back in where we left off, spending more time together than ever. Although I'm not falling in love the way I fell for Ryne, I do feel myself falling a different way. With Ryne, love felt like an exhilarating free fall, but with Bell, it's like jumping—I just have to make that choice to step off the edge into the unknown. Because of him, I'm changing. My heart is opening. Most of all, my mind is accepting that I could have a different life with Bell, a happy one. Maybe even a better one as long as we don't have to be around Ryne.

Except for one problem—Bellamy doesn't know the real me.

He doesn't know that I'm a lycan or that I'm not a virgin, both things that could be non-negotiable for a beta wolf shifter in search of a wife. Faye insists I should take these secrets to my grave, and Elle says Bell deserves the truth, that he's a good guy and will accept me for me.

But I don't know.

My palms sweat, and my knee won't stop bouncing as we sit at dinner in his manor one warm September night. It's become one of my favorite dates with him, to join him and several of the mating-house women here. Now that I know Abi is okay, at least for now, I can talk to these women without the incredible guilt I had the first time he brought me here.

"What's wrong?" Bellamy asks, steadying my knee. His large hand is warm and comforting, but I'm still beyond nervous. "Is the food not to your liking? You've barely touched it."

I stare down at the full plate of cold food and sigh, knowing I can't keep these secrets another day. We're together too much, he wants me too much, and things are progressing without the truth. It's time. If he hates me for it, then so be it. If he tries to have me executed, I should have enough allies around to hopefully save my life and get me to the panther sanctuary. But if he accepts me, if he really is okay with all of me, lycan and everything, then maybe it's time to let myself love him the way he deserves. To make that leap.

"Can we go somewhere and talk?" I ask.

"Outside?"

"More private." As much as his yard seems private, there are neighbors, and I can't take any risks with this information. This has to be just him and me. Though, in some ways I'm risking my life that way too. He might try to kill me. It's a risk I have to take.

His lovely green eyes widen, and he stands, taking my hand and leading me into a wing of the house I haven't been in before. "All the bedrooms are occupied, and I can't guarantee privacy in the common areas. Is it okay that we go to my bedroom?"

I swallow hard and nod. "I need to talk to you about something," I reiterate. "It's nothing more—"

He squeezes my hand to cut me off. "I'd never assume anything was going to happen between us before marriage, and I swear I won't try."

That stings a little, but I trust him enough to take him at his word and follow him into the large room. It's more modest than the rest of the house, not what I expected, but I kind of love it. He has a large bed with a white comforter, an oak dresser, and a closed door that probably leads to a private bathroom. I sit on the edge of the bed and then think better of it and stand, pacing from one side of the room to the other.

"Are you okay?" Concern laces his tone. Only concern. Not suspicion. Not expectation. And not judgment. He's such a good man.

This is it. Now or never.

I turn to him. "I'm not who you think I am."

His smile quirks. "And who are you then?" He stands and approaches. I don't move, allowing him to tuck a strand of hair behind my ear and cup my face gently. "Because I'm pretty sure I have a good idea by now, and I'll tell you, I like you, Poppy. A lot."

"I'm not a virgin," I blurt out, expecting him to flinch away from me like I've just burned him.

He only shrugs. "I figured you weren't, knowing the way Ryne looks at you." He clears his throat. "And I know you were taken by lone wolves. I figured they might have . . ."

"I've only been with Ryne," I say quickly. "And you're okay with that? I thought betas required that wives come to them virginal."

"Some do, and some women would prefer it that way too, but it's not important to me." He peers into my eyes. "I care about your heart, your tenacity, and your drive—all things that matter way more to me than your virginity."

Relief floods me, but it's short-lived. "There's one more thing."

One more big thing. One more thing that could ruin us forever, that could make him see me as a monster. Make him hate me.

"What is it?" He arches a brow. "I can take it."

Oh, I'm not sure you can, Bell.

I step back and wring my hands. This is not going to go over nearly as well as the virginity confession. But he doesn't let me stay there. He steps forward, placing his hand on my cheek again. He wants to reassure me, to make me feel like I can trust him, but there's no way he's expecting I'm a monster—his greatest enemy. I take a deep breath and proceed. "When I was kidnapped, it wasn't by lone wolves. It was by the lycan. I was with a pack of lycan for three whole months before I was rescued."

He nods slowly, his eyes creasing in alarm. "And if I ever catch the bastards who took you, I'll kill them for what they did."

I wince. "Except, they didn't *take* me. They took me in. I had been banished when they caught me in the wilds."

He freezes at that, his warm hand still cupping my cheek. It doesn't move, but I expect it will with what I say next. "I had been bitten by one of them during the blood moon attack. Ryne sent me away for it instead of killing me."

His lips part, but besides that, he's still frozen.

"So you see, I'm one of them now. I'm a lycan."

CHAPTER 18

JUST AS I EXPECTED, Bellamy's hand drops from my face, and he sinks down onto the edge of his bed. He stares at the floor, not saying a word. I shouldn't be surprised, but his reaction doesn't hurt as much as I feared.

If this were Ryne, I'd be right next to him, begging him to understand, to love me, to want me. But this isn't Ryne. It's Bellamy, and as much as I like him, I don't love him yet. If this is a deal breaker for him, I'll understand. And I won't even be angry. How could I blame him for rejecting me? Any other wolf would. Even my own mate did in the end.

He finally glances up at me, and his eyes are a little haunted. "What does that mean for us?"

It's not the question I was planning to answer. "What do you mean?"

"You could kill me on the full moon."

"I could, but I can control my lycan form, so I'm not worried about hurting anyone. And I'll keep to myself; no wolves will ever see me. Oh, and kissing is off-limits three days before and after."

"You know this because of Ryne?" His fists clench on the bed's comforter.

"Yes. Kissing would cause him to pass out."

His fists clench even harder. "Thinking of that bastard kissing you always makes me see red."

I crease my eyebrows together. "I thought you liked Ryne."

"I do. He's my alpha. But I hate what he did to you, and the thought of you two together kills me. And sometimes . . . sometimes, I think maybe I hate him."

Unfortunately, I know the feeling.

I know Bell likes me, but to hate his own alpha on my behalf, to call him a bastard? It's everything I need at this moment, the kind of validation that I haven't gotten from a man before. Not ever.

And it feels so good.

"Tell me something," Bellamy asks in a low voice. "If Ryne was willing to be with you even though he knew you were a lycan, what changed?"

I swallow. This I cannot tell. Ryne has kept this from his wolves for good reason. Who knows how they'll react? Maybe they'll rise up and kill him for it, or maybe they won't, but either way, it's his secret to share when he's ready.

"We had a fight about how to handle the Resistance,

and he decided that he'd be better off with a luna." I hate lying to Bell, but it's close enough to the truth. And honestly, Ryne abandoning me for accidentally biting him isn't fair. He may as well have dumped me for a luna.

Bellamy approaches me again and, to my surprise, slides a hand behind my back, tugging me close to him. He rests his forehead on mine. "You're lying. I can tell, but that's okay. I'm guessing you're hiding something for him. You being a lycan definitely makes things more complicated for us, but I don't care, Poppy. I want you to be mine, and I'll be there for you, no matter what."

Then he smashes his lips against mine. I return the kiss eagerly, grateful for his instant acceptance of who I am. I'm a lycan who is not a virgin and who is fated to someone else, and he still wants me. Against all the odds, we're here together. Choosing each other. Jumping together.

And maybe that's better than fate.

We tumble onto his bed, and the kissing goes beyond what we've done before, our bodies exploring each other. We don't have sex, but it's only a matter of time if things progress. I fall into the warmth of his skin, the strength of his long, lean muscles, and the taste of his mouth. We're wrapped up in a fiery heat. It's not as hot as it was with Ryne, but it doesn't burn me either. It's just enough to keep me safe and make me feel loved.

Suddenly, he pulls away, breathing heavily. "I should take you home."

I collapse back onto his bed, my own feelings of desire swirling. "Or I could just stay. I'm not ready to give myself to you yet, but that doesn't mean we can't share a bed. It's late."

I want to stay here, for me and for him. And a voice in my head also wants Ryne to hear about it. He hurt me, so why shouldn't I hurt him too?

Bell chuckles and slides a hand across my stomach. "It's not that late, but I will not turn down that offer. I promise to be good." But the devilish way he says "good" tells me he'd be open for more if I was too. He drops his head to my neck and kisses it slowly, working his way to my collarbone. I weave my fingers through his thick hair and lose myself in the sensations.

This is definitely better than going home and worrying about everything, and I realize, in this moment, exactly why I like Bellamy. He not only makes me feel safe, but I trust him with every fiber of my being. If he says he's going to be good, he'll be good. When I'm with him, I don't have to be Poppy—the savior of the Resistance, or Poppy—the fearsome lycan, or Poppy—the rejected mate. I'm just a normal girl who enjoys kissing and cuddling, who wants to be wanted, to be loved, the same as everyone else.

THE NEXT MORNING, I wake in Bellamy's arms. I know I should go home, but I want to stay here forever and be the mistress of the house that helps the girls in the mating houses. I could be so much more effective here. I don't need more classes or lunas glaring at me. I don't need to date around or watch my fated mate fall for someone else.

This is what I need.

"Morning, gorgeous," Bellamy says, his voice raspy from sleep. I jerk my head around. I hadn't realized he was awake.

"Good morning." I cuddle even closer to him.

"We should get you back."

"I've been thinking about that. What if I don't want to go back? I could just stay here with you and help you with the girls."

He tightens his grip on me. "As much as I'd love that, Madame Delphine needs you for the Resistance, and I don't want to cross her."

I shake my head at that. "She wants what's best for me as much as she wants what's best for the other women. I'm sure she'd agree that I should stay here if it makes me happy. I can still help the Resistance from here."

His lips thin as he rakes a hand through that unruly hair of his. "And what about Ryne? You really think he'll just let you move in with me?"

I shrug and sit up. "Ryne doesn't get a say in my life anymore."

"Except that he does. He has to approve all the beta marriages, and it's going to be hard enough to get him to agree to us being together." His face stills, and he studies me for a long minute, neither of us saying anything.

"Why would he disagree with us being together? I thought that's what he wanted. It's what he told everyone."

Bellamy gives a dark chuckle. "Sure he did. But as soon as he saw that you and I were getting close, he had words with me."

My eyebrows rise. I hadn't heard about this. "And what exactly were those words?"

"He told me to back off. That he had changed his mind about you marrying a beta."

My body goes cold and hot all at once. "He can go to hell."

"He'll never approve of our marriage. I know I should've told you before." He gives a sheepish grin. "But I was afraid you'd go running back to him."

I grab his hand. "I'm not. It's you I want." Even as I say the words, I'm still not convinced that they're true.

"I could challenge him for alpha. That would solve all of this."

Tears blur my vision. "That's the last thing I want because one of you would die, and it would be my fault."

"One of us would die," he agrees, "but it wouldn't be your fault. None of this is your fault. Still, I couldn't do that to you. And honestly, I don't want to challenge Ryne, and I have no interest in being the alpha, at least, not in this pack. I'd only fight for it if I had to, and I don't think I do."

"I still believe Ryne will do the right thing when the alpha king is named, but if he doesn't, let someone else fight him." But the thought of someone else, anyone else, hurting Ryne makes me want to burst into tears.

"It's okay, Poppy. We only have to wait a little longer, and then I can choose you as my bride at the harvest festival. If Ryne doesn't agree, we'll run away together."

"If Ryne agrees, then what happens?" My voice cracks.

"Then you decide what comes next. We can stay here and keep doing what we're doing, helping the mating-house women, or we can go out west and join that other pack I told you about. Either way, I promise to keep you safe." He shifts in bed until he's sitting across from me, taking my hands between his. "But I want you to be mine. I don't want to watch you wish you were with another man. Do you ever think you'll be able to give him up?"

As I'm confronted with the question, panic grips me, but I force myself to calm and squeeze his hands back. Then I answer the question I have no business answering. "Yes," I say softly. And then more forcefully. "Yes."

CHAPTER 19

"YOU SLEPT WITH HIM."

It's the first sentence Ryne has spoken to me in more than two weeks. I'm out on my morning run by myself after having returned from Bell's house, sweat dripping down my face and lungs burning in my chest.

I whip around to find Ryne standing a few feet away from me. He's completely naked, covered in dirt, with a murderous expression etched onto his rugged face. His dark hair hangs around his shoulders, tangled and windswept. He hasn't looked this unkempt since the wilds. And his eyes—his eyes are as bright blue as I've ever seen them.

"Where are your clothes?" I squeak. It appears he shifted and ran all the way over here this morning instead of driving like normal.

He doesn't answer my question as he stalks in close.

He catches my face in his hand and forces me to look into his savage gaze. "Did you have sex with him?" he asks.

I swallow hard, my heart pounding in my chest. I knew this confrontation could be a possibility if I stayed with Bellamy last night. I knew it, and I stayed anyway because I wanted to see Ryne angry and jealous. Why should I have to sit around and watch him move on with somebody new while he's telling Bellamy to back off from me? Love works both ways, and so does heartbreak.

"That's none of your business," I spit.

"The hell it isn't." He runs his nose along my neck, and goosebumps erupt, memories flooding of the last time he did something like that. "You smell like him. You reek of lust."

"We didn't have sex!" I grind out and snap back, pushing him off me. "But we're going to soon, and there's not a damn thing you can do about it. You dumped me, remember?"

His cold eyes burn into a raging inferno. "And it was a mistake!"

Those words pierce through my heart, but I don't let them stay for long. I'll deal with the wound later. "And what about dating the lunas? That a mistake too? Or do you have another one lined up for tonight, same as all the other nights?"

"I want you back," he states. "I don't care about the lunas. I never did."

"And why should I believe you? You've put me through more than enough heartbreak already. Bellamy treats me like a queen. You treated me like a burden."

He winces, but I don't take it back. It's true. He knows it's true.

"You are not to have sex again until you're married," he says at last, as if he has any right to tell me what to do with my body. "And if you still want him, come time for the harvest moon proposals, then so be it."

"And what if I don't wait? Would you stop wanting me back if I have sex with someone else?"

"No matter what you do or where you go or who you're with, I will always want you," he growls. His face softens, and he inches closer to me. I stand motionless as his hands run up my arms to cup my face. I'm very much aware that he's naked right now. "I love you, Poppy."

"You have a funny way of showing it."

"I'm sorry—"

"How long until the Harvest Moon Festival?" I interrupt.

He blinks, surprised. "Six weeks, give or take a day."

I rip myself away, and it's like ripping my heart in two all over again. "Fine. What's another six weeks to wait for Bellamy, a man who has loved me from day one with his *actions* and not just his *words*?"

And then I turn and sprint away, hoping that I can make it six weeks without crumbling under the pressure of such a huge decision. Because as much as I adore

Bellamy, I'm still hopelessly in love with Ryne, but I meant what I said. Actions matter more to me now than ever. Words be damned.

I RETURN to my room and find both Faye and Elle sitting on my bed, giggling about something. Faye had been asleep when I'd changed into my workout clothes this morning, and it still catches me off guard sometimes to see her being so nice to my friends. But it's nice. Really nice, actually.

Elle meets my gaze. "So. Here we thought you spent the night at Bellamy's and were both ready to milk you for every detail, but I think this is even juicier."

"I did stay at Bellamy's."

Faye gapes. "Girl. You've some nerve." She drops her voice. "Are you sleeping with both of them?"

"Both of whom?"

Elle points to the window. "We saw you and Ryne at the edge of the woods."

"I've never seen him naked. That is one fine man." Faye fans her face. "Please tell me Bellamy is just as hot."

"Faye. What about Justin?"

"What about him?"

Faye flushes. "I haven't seen him naked."

"Wait a minute, you two aren't sleeping together?"

Elle asks. "Because you sure have made it sound like you are."

"Yeah, in front of the other women because they need to back off my man." Faye winks. "Justin wants to wait until after we're married. So I have to live vicariously through Miss I'm-sleeping-with-two-incredibly-hot-wolves."

I drop down onto Faye's bed and face them. My shower will have to wait. It might be good for me to get out my messy emotions.

"Bellamy and I aren't having sex, but I did spend the night with him. And Ryne and I aren't back together, but he wants to be."

Elle blinks at me for a moment. "We need more details than that."

I spill everything to them, including Ryne's secret since they already know I bit him and that he survived. They can be trusted. And they are surprisingly good listeners. It's almost as good as talking with Joanna or Willow.

Once the story is all out, I wait.

"I think you should get back together with Ryne. You know it's going to happen anyway. Why postpone the inevitable?" Faye says matter-of-factly.

"No way. Ryne's an asshole. He didn't want her back until she was with someone else. Someone that makes her happy. She deserves someone like Bellamy." Elle crosses her arms and glares at Faye.

"Excuse me, Miss Elle." I point at her. "You've been

team Ryne since the second you found out we were fated. What changed?"

"What's changed is Ryne hurt you, and Bellamy put you back together. Bell's a really good man."

"But he's not her mate," Faye points out.

They bicker back and forth about who I should be with, and I find that I like this. My friends are amazing. If nothing else, I've learned that bonds with women are stronger than my messed-up relationships. I still can't believe Faye and I went from hating to trusting each other, but here we are. I don't know if I'll ever forget the things she said about Willow or the way she blackmailed me in the wilds, but things are different between us. I've forgiven her. Not that she asked—she's still not the type to ask for forgiveness or apologize for anything.

"You don't know what you're talking about," Faye argues. "You don't have a fated mate."

"Neither do you."

"That's what I'm telling you. I've seen fated relationships. Look at Shauna and Amos. There's no breaking that bond. Look at Nico and Nova. Look at Joanna and Grady. She abandoned all of us just to be with him. Joanna. The strongest of all of us. You can't break the fated bonds. Ryne didn't come back to Poppy because he got jealous of Bellamy. He came back to her because he can't live without her, and Poppy's eventually going to realize that she can't live without him either. It's not fair to put Bellamy through that. Surely, even you can see that."

No one says anything for a long moment. Then Elle meets my eye. "I think she's right."

I grit my teeth and grab my clothes out of my dresser then storm into the shower.

That's not what I want to hear.

CHAPTER 20

AT LUNCH, Faye sits down with a silly grin on her face. "Guess where Justin is taking me on our date tonight?"

"Where?" I ask, glad to be talking about her love life instead of mine.

"We're going to look at houses."

"Houses?"

"Yeah. You know, for after we're married? He said we can stay at his, or we can choose a different one. He wants it to be our house. I'm so excited."

"That sounds super fun." I'll admit it took me a while to accept that Justin was serious about Faye, or that she wasn't just using him. They've both surprised me, and I can't help but wonder how the other women feel about it. Are they happy for Faye, or do they secretly want to take Justin away?

"What are you and Bellamy doing tonight?" Samantha turns to me with a sad crease between her eyes. She hasn't made a solid connection with any of the betas. Even Lev hasn't given her the time of day. She liked Dante, but since his death, she's been thinking more about The Sanctuary. The schooling part of our time here isn't what it used to be, which was where she thrived. Now that it's all about dating, I can't say I blame her.

I shake my thoughts free and refocus on her question. "It's Elle's night with him."

"We're just having dinner at his place and hanging out with the girls from the mating houses, same as always," Elle cuts in. "You can come along if you want, Poppy. You know he'd rather be with you anyway."

"That sounds like fun." I shrug. I had planned to do some reading in bed tonight, but I do like Bell's place, and it's always great to have Elle around. She gets along so well with everyone.

"Boring." Violet snorts from where she's sitting with the other lunas. I'll admit I haven't made an effort to befriend them, but they haven't either. They still act like we're beneath them.

Faye shoots her a wicked glare. "What? Do you have something to say?"

I bristle, wishing Faye didn't have to be so . . . Faye. Now that she's decided we're friends, she's turned her vitriol toward the three lunas who are eligible to date. And although Cecily and Marissa haven't been a basket of fun, she hates Violet the most. Not that I like Violet with her nose-in-the-air attitude, but still, those girls can turn into scary, fearsome wolves.

And Faye? That girl is more bark than bite.

"As a matter of fact, I do," Violet announces. "Last night, I went to Ryne and demanded that the lunas get better treatment from the betas. You're all acting as if you're already engaged, but you're not."

"I thought you didn't want a beta," Faye retorts.

Violet shrugs. "Maybe, maybe not, but I'm tired of sitting around while you humans have all the fun." She fluffs her hair.

"Haven't you been out with Ryne lately? Or did he get sick of you?" Samantha asks, and Violet's face turns almost as red as her hair.

"He's not dating anyone right now. He's decided he's too busy with pack stuff."

That makes my cheeks prickle, and everyone looks at me expectantly. "What?" I blurt. "Ryne and I aren't together. You know that."

"Anyway," Violet cuts back in sharply. "Ryne assured me that things are changing, and I'll have all the dates I can dream of with the other betas. Marissa here has already got Lev drooling all over her." That's news to me, but nobody else seems surprised by it. She points her fingers at me and Faye. "Which means you two better watch out because Cecily and I are coming for Bellamy and Justin."

Marissa is completely unaffected by this conversation, eating her lunch as if it's not even happening, but

Cecily has a smug grin on her face. She's excited for the challenge—in fact, she wants nothing more than to take us down.

Faye smirks. "Good luck with that."

But I don't smirk. I don't like this, not one bit. The lunas don't have much to lose, not like we remaining humans do. What if the betas can't resist the lunas' charms? We'll be sent to the mating houses if we can't get to The Sanctuary in time. Right now it's still a possibility, but things can change quickly here, and someday our safe haven may be gone.

I SPEND the night at Bellamy's again.

And the next.

And the next.

We don't get close to having sex, but we do thoroughly enjoy each other. He brings me home early each morning, and each morning, Ryne is hiding in the shadows of the woods, watching. Ryne doesn't run off anymore, but I don't go over to talk to him either. We're at an impasse.

Faye and Elle don't say much about the situation anymore, but I know they disapprove. Even now that Bellamy has to date the other women, and I have to date the other men, he still has me come over at night. And I always go. Maybe I shouldn't, maybe Faye and Elle are right to judge me, maybe Bell is using me—more likely

I'm using him, but my heart is too broken not to try to fix it. I keep expecting Madame Delphine or Ryne to put a stop to our sleepovers, but they never do. It's as if Ryne is finally letting me make my own choices . . . I'm not sure how to feel about that.

"Excuse me, ladies," Madame Delphine announces one afternoon while we're in the middle of a particularly excruciating singing lesson. We all jerk our heads toward her, and the room goes eerily silent. "Ryne has called a pack-wide meeting. It will be at seven o'clock tonight at the arena. He wants us all there. Please wear a nice dress, but no need to be fancy. We will eat before we leave in case it goes late. Any dates for tonight will be postponed to tomorrow."

She gives a quick nod and then leaves the room.

"See?" Violet is the first to speak. "This is what I've been saying. Things are changing around here."

Elle, Faye, and I all stare at each other. Then we all scramble up and go after Madame Delphine. I reach her first before she escapes into her office. "What's the meeting about?" I ask more forcefully than I meant.

"I have no idea. It's with the entire pack except those who are out on guard duty. Whatever it is, it's big."

"Do you think we have a new alpha king?" Elle asks. Her eyes drift away, and I know her father is on her mind. It makes me want to give her a big hug.

"That's what I'm thinking, but I'm not positive." Madame Delphine wrings her hands.

The doorknob on the front door jiggles, and I jump.

We all move back a few inches, and the door swings open. I expect it to be anyone but who it is.

Joanna.

She stands there, staring at all of us, her eyes wild, her hair tangled.

"I need help," she says.

And then she collapses into my arms, sobbing.

CHAPTER 21

SEEING Joanna again is a total shock. I squeeze her tightly as Madame Delphine ushers us into the office, Elle and Faye slipping in as well. Joanna sinks to the floor in the middle of the room, and I sink with her, refusing to let her go. She's unkempt, even more so than when I saw her in the wilds, and has cuts and bruises that look fresh. Her glossy eyes dart around to each of us as she murmurs a string of unintelligible nonsense. She's hyperventilating so hard that we can't understand her.

"Take a deep breath," I coach. "Look at me, talk to me, just me."

Her gaze holds mine, and I recognize the heartache and panic there—it's the same look I saw in the mirror my first night in the manor.

Something happened.

Something bad.

"Is it Grady?" I whisper and then hold my breath,

waiting for the bad news that is surely coming, but she shakes her head.

"Grady is in hiding," she says. "He's alive. It's not Grady. It's my parents."

"What happened to them?"

"They're going to be kidnapped at the next full moon. Laik is still targeting the villages, and when I tried to reason with him, he said he would go get my parents next. And then he attacked me. Grady nearly died defending me. That's when we fled."

"Does Laik know you're here?" Elle interrupts, her voice on edge.

Joanna blinks at her but shakes her head. "We ran off in the opposite direction and then doubled back down here."

"That was smart," Madame Delphine says. "If Laik suspects we know his plans, he'll change them."

"He's gone completely rogue," Elle adds. "His crew is no longer with the Resistance."

"I know." Joanna nods, a dazed and horrified look coming over her face.

"And yet you and your mate went with them." Faye throws her hands in the air and widens her eyes at me. "Am I going to be the only one to say it? You can't trust her. This could be a trap."

"It's not," Joanna cries out. "If you won't help the humans, who will? The full moon is coming up, and Laik has more lycans now than ever."

"And yet you're not a lycan," Faye challenges. "Or are you? How would we even know?"

"She's *not* a lycan," I cut in, but nobody seems to care what I have to say.

Joanna glares at Faye and then addresses Madame Delphine. "What is she even doing here? Get her out."

"I'm with the Resistance now, actually," Faye huffs. "Which is more than you can say, considering your recent actions."

Elle says nothing, Madame Delphine appears conflicted, and Faye is out for blood.

"Enough." I stand and bring Joanna up with me, keeping my arm around her. "Joanna is one of our own, and if she needs help, then we're going to help her."

"That's not up to you to decide," Madame Delphine says with a resolute sigh. "But we can go to Ryne and ask for help."

I'm not sure where Ryne's feelings are going to fall on this. I know he was upset that his guards were killed. I know he hates Laik. But Joanna and Grady made their choice . . .

"I promise I'm not a lycan," Joanna tries. "Ryne can trust me."

"I'm not so sure he'll see it that way." Madame Delphine sighs.

Joanna stiffens, and I speak up. "If Ryne won't help you, I will. I know what went down at the last full moon, Joanna, because I was there. I saw you. I know you're still human, and I know you're not with Laik anymore."

"That was you?" she asks, and I take the time to explain to everyone what I saw that night.

"Don't you see? Joanna doesn't support stealing someone's agency like that. We should protect her."

"That's not up to us," Faye says. She's still prickly and not wanting to soften up. "That's up to Ryne."

I turn to Joanna, tuning everyone else out. "Don't worry. I won't let anything happen to you or your family."

"You promise?"

"I swear on my life."

THE STADIUM IS PACKED with wolves. I'm reminded of the last time I was here, when the wolves were fighting for dominance and rank, even to the death. And then I met Thorn, who wanted me sent to the mating house for his enjoyment. Thorn, who nearly ruined his son's life. Thorn, whose death I thought would mean the end of the mating houses. I bristle and push the memories aside because he's dead, and I'm stronger now.

One small section is left unoccupied and is guarded by a few beta wolves, keeping people out. Madame Delphine guides us down to that section, and we sit in the very front row. Faye sits between Elle and me. Once the meeting is over, we're going to Ryne's house to see what he can do about Joanna's family and village. For now, she's hiding out at the manor, probably worried sick, but at least, she's safe.

Ryne is nowhere to be seen. Once everyone is settled, anticipation crackles through the air. The door behind the section where we are sitting opens, and Justin and Bellamy walk in. They hold the doors wide, and a woman walks through, followed by several others. A hush falls over the stadium. They walk down the stairs and sit in the rows behind us. I stare at them and realize these are the women from the mating houses. I recognize several from my nights out at Bell's house, but there are far more than I even knew.

Eventually, a very pregnant woman comes through the door, followed by others with baby bumps of various sizes. My heart leaps when I catch sight of Abi. She's starting to show. There are too many people, so I doubt she can see me, but I watch as she navigates the bleachers and sits down. Ryne is the last one in.

He looks happier than I've seen him in a long time. His hair is tied back, his eyes are clear, and there is a light smile on his lips.

Once he hits the ground, he picks up a microphone, his eyes locking on mine for a long, tense moment before roaming the crowd.

A hush falls over the arena before he speaks. "Wolves and women, I'm sure you are curious why I brought you here. Tonight, some of you are going to hear things you don't like, but I'll not apologize for it." My heart speeds, and I grip the edge of my seat as he takes command. “Things need to change, and I’ve been reluctant to make these changes because I’ve been afraid of the consequences. As the new alpha king remains undecided, and the wolf kingdom grows more unstable by the day, I’m choosing to run our pack independently. We may or may not align ourselves with the new king, depending on his goals.”

Murmurs ripple among the crowd, but I just want them to shut up so that I can hear what else he has to say.

“I understand that what I’m about to announce will displease some of you. If you wish to leave the pack, you are free to go. There are many packs that will continue with old traditions, and if those appeal to you, we will not come after you.”

I’m hanging onto his every word, hope igniting within my soul.

Is this it? Is this finally the end?

“The mating houses have been a tradition among our people since the virus mutated our fertility after the great wars. We were a dying race, and we had to take action to correct that. But now we are thriving, thanks to the many women who have sacrificed their freedom unwillingly.” He gives the many women a slight nod, and a few of them bristle while others perk up. “I recognize that this is not something that will be easily changed overnight, but effective immediately, the mating houses as you know them no longer exist in the Carolina Pack.”

The rumbling increases, and I’m dumbfounded.

Faye grips my hand, and Elle meets my eye. "He's doing this for you," she whispers.

Maybe Elle's right, but I don't think so. He talked about this before. He's doing this because he knows it's the right thing to do, and he's planned this out for a long time. He was waiting for the alpha king to be established, but if he's right, that the kingdom is growing unstable, then now is the perfect way to set his pack apart from the rest. And doing it quickly makes it harder for people to plan counter moves against him.

They're either with him, or they're not.

"You can't do that," someone shouts angrily.

"I can, and I will," Ryne snaps back, his voice echoing through the stadium. "This is the first opportunity you have to leave if you wish. I will explain how this will be done, and you will likely still get as much sex as you want, but right now, if you refuse, you will no longer be welcome here. Anyone who wishes to leave may do so now. The Capital City Pack is the closest geographically, but I expect if you really want your pick of mating houses, you'll have to head to Chicago and fight for alpha king yourself."

That shuts everyone up.

The king still hasn't been decided because every time someone rises to power, they're immediately killed. It's a bloodbath up there.

Ryne clears his throat. "I've spoken with the alphas of the surrounding packs, and they are willing to accept you if Carolina is no longer to be your home." The man is serious, maybe more so than I've ever seen him before, as his calm demeanor turns thunderous. "If you're going to go, you need to go now. Don't look back!"

Silence descends. Then a handful of wolves get up and start to leave, then a few more. Then a stampede starts.

Ryne just lost half his pack within minutes.

But most of his betas are still by his side, protecting him, loyal as ever.

I would be uneasy about the loss of the wolves, but I'm too flooded with excitement. And I'm not the only one—every single woman in the stadium has an expression of either stunned disbelief, immense relief, or knowing satisfaction. This is the day we've all been praying for, hoping for, *fighting* for.

"Some of you might feel that we are weakened now, but I disagree. We just lost half of the pack who aren't willing to fight for what is right, and that is what I intend to do. We will fight to make a better life for all of us. Now that those who are not willing to adapt have left, I will explain exactly what I'm planning. But first, a story.

"A young delta wolf came to me several weeks ago and explained that he had fallen in love. That is a privilege that right now is afforded only to betas, though it is my understanding that at some of the mating houses, something like monogamy does occur. Unfortunately, the woman he is in love with is not in one of those houses. I visited with her a couple of days ago, and she confirmed the story the delta told me. She's absolutely in love with him. And so, the first change that will take place is that any wolf—regardless of place in the pack—is allowed to take a wife or girlfriend. This must be a consensual relationship. You are not allowed to take a woman home and keep her if she doesn't want to go. This will take place immediately."

A squeal erupts a few rows behind me, and a woman crawls over all the others, shoves past the betas guarding them, and flings herself into the arms of a man a couple of sections over. Then a half-dozen more women do the same.

It shifts the energy in the stadium, and Faye snorts under her breath, but she's also grinning.

"A couple of other changes will take place immediately as well. Women will be allowed to raise any children they bear." At this, several women start audibly sobbing, and Ryne has to speak up to be heard over them. "They can give children up to the pack if they wish them to be raised as they are now, but if not, all women will be given a safe place to raise their children alone or with a partner. These children will still be required to attend daily classes with the others but will go home at night to their mothers."

This is huge.

None of these wolves, save for the betas, were raised this way. Not in this pack, and as far as I know, not in the entire wolf shifter kingdom. Everyone stares at Ryne as if he's just grown a second head, but I look at him like he's the man I always knew he could be.

And I'm so damn proud.

"All claimed men and women will be compensated for their labors, and you wolves will have to pay for services yourselves, whatever it is you want from the claimed, be it sex or labor. Effective immediately, all sex will be consensual, and all sex in the mating houses will be fairly compensated. And all my shifters will be receiving wage increases to meet the demand."

That sends a wave of whispers through the crowd, and people aren't so uneasy anymore. This can work. I know it can work.

"Women can choose to use this money to help their families back home in the villages, or they can spend it on themselves or on whatever else they desire. The pack will still provide free lodging in the mating houses should you choose to stay there." He turns to the women, smiling gently. "But if you would like, you may go home." Even more women burst into tears, and my own vision blurs. "Tell your villages that all adult human men and women are welcome to come work in the wolf city for a better life, but we will also be taking measures to ensure a better quality of life out in the villages and hope most humans will stay put. We will continue to protect the villages during the full moons."

I hope that's true because the lycans are only getting stronger, and I have a feeling Laik isn't going to stop, no matter how many changes Ryne makes. As wonderful as all this is, those lycans want the wolves dead and gone. It's as simple as that.

"Actual relationships used to be our way of life, and it is my intention that we return to it." Ryne's eyes quickly flash to mine before moving on. "But since we need to keep growing the pack, the mating houses will stay open, and my hope is that they will continue to be fruitful for generations." He motions to the betas, and most of the ones who are left stand up. "I've already recruited many of my betas who are prepared to enforce our new laws."

Bellamy is one of them.

His green gaze meets mine—his eyes are brimming with determination, with the love he feels for me, the life we've talked about, and I no longer know what to do. Now that Ryne is making these changes, can I forgive him? Take him back? Or have I already moved on?

CHAPTER 22

RYNE IS SWARMED WITH QUESTIONS, prolonging the meeting well into the night, and we decide not to go to his house to bombard him with the news from Joanna. I expect to be wired by the time we get back to the manor, but as soon as my head hits the pillow, I fall into a deep sleep.

I wake to a soft knock on the door and sit up as Faye rolls over and covers her head with a pillow. Long auburn curls stick up at odd angles against the backdrop of her fluffy white blankets, and I smile to myself. I pad to the door and open it to find a disheveled Bellamy.

And I don't know how to feel about seeing him.

"Hi," I croak. "What are you doing here?"

He takes my hand. "Can we talk?"

I agree, and he leads me out into the quiet sitting room. The soft morning sunrise filters through the curtains, and we sit down next to each other on the sofa.

"You didn't come over last night," he states.

"The announcements went late, and I figured you'd be busy helping enforce everything."

His lips curve into a satisfied smile. "I was."

"How did it go?"

"Better than expected," he says, and then those expressive eyes darken. "It helped that Ryne sent so many of the wolves away like that. They're probably halfway to new packs by now, and good riddance."

It's not enough that the other packs are still going to carry on as if things don't need to change, but maybe our pack can be the start of a revolution.

I've never thought of it as our pack until now.

"Any dissenters?" I ask.

He nods. "Some of the betas, as we expected."

"Why's that?"

"Pack loyalty is stronger for betas. Most of us had to fight our way to this rank, and some of us have wives and families. Leaving isn't so easy. They don't want to start over somewhere else when they're happy and well established already."

"So they can pay for their prostitutes," I snap. "They'll still get plenty of sex."

"They don't want to start paying for something that they've always gotten for free. Besides, there will be fewer women to choose from now. These men are going to have to start respecting the women that do stay, and I don't think some of our betas know the meaning of the word."

He's right. I hate that some of those men regularly visit the mating houses even though they're married. A trickle of fear goes through me, and I wonder how many of them are going to make a play for Ryne's alpha position. If someone takes him down, everything could go back to the way it was—or worse.

Bell squeezes my hand. "Hey, don't worry. Things are changing, and that's what matters."

I gaze at our hands and look back up at him. "You're right. I just still can't believe it. I think I'm in shock."

His eyes search mine. "I want to kiss you so badly right now, but I know I can't."

I frown at that. "Because?"

"Because the full moon is in three days, and we can't risk it." Oh, yeah. Right. *That.* "But if there wasn't the full moon coming up, would you want me to kiss you after last night?"

That's the question of the day, and it would be so easy to say yes to him, but I have to be honest. He deserves the truth. We both do.

"I'm confused," I whisper. "I don't know what to do."

His face falls, but he doesn't release my hand. "I expected that. It's okay. You don't have to make a decision now, but I meant what I said before. I need to know you want me and only me if we're getting engaged at the festival next month."

The fact that we're still having a festival at all was one of the questions from last night. I don't like it. As far as I'm concerned, we should be done with everything having to do with the claiming. But the beta wolves insisted that it makes sense to still hold it since we're already so close to the engagements. And Ryne announced that next year's claiming will be on a voluntary basis—an opportunity for human women over the age of eighteen to date betas for a year, to learn about pack life and what it means to be a beta's wife, without the fear of the mating houses.

Some of the lower ranks wanted to know if they could join the claiming to find a wife as well, and Ryne said he'd consider it. I'm not even sure what that would look like. It's hard to imagine. How many more women would there need to be? And how many more men would sign up? It's still an unanswered question. Something like that would've saved Knox before it was too late.

Although allowing the claimed men and women to carry on here isn't my preference, I'm okay with it. These changes certainly would've made the last year of my life a million times better.

But again, it's all too late.

I walk Bellamy out. He didn't bring his car today but rode in on his boat instead. He kisses me gently on the cheek before motoring off down the river. I sit down on the bank and lie in the tall grass, my silk pajamas soft on my skin and the canopy of trees for cover.

Some of the trees are starting to change colors already, a few of the green leaves giving way to hues of yellow and orange. I'm reminded of my first date with Ryne, of riding that horse out to the forest, his body pressed to mine. Of climbing the tree and all the red leaves that surrounded us when he tried to kiss me for the first time, and I refused him.

So much has changed—and yet here we are, right back where we started.

Him wanting me—and me not feeling sure I can trust him.

"So that's it, huh?" Ryne's voice breaks me from my daydreams, and I jump up to find him standing tall a few feet away. His hands are stuffed into the pockets of the same clothing he wore yesterday. His hair is still tied back, though bits of it have pulled free to frame his face, and his eyes are red from weeks without proper sleep.

"What's it?" I ask.

"You're choosing Bell." It's not a question. It's a statement.

"I don't know." I throw my hands up. "We've already discussed this, Ryne. I have until the harvest moon to make my decision."

He inches closer. "You asked me to show you my true feelings for you with my actions, so I have. Can't you see I'm fighting for you here? That I love you? That I'm sorry?"

"That's the thing. Did you do this just for me? If so, that's not enough."

Ryne jabs a hand through his hair. "No. I didn't do it just for you. I was planning on doing it anyway but was waiting for the alpha king to be chosen before deciding how I was going to make this work. But I did do it early just for you. I want to prove to you that I'm the man you deserve. Poppy, you cannot deny this." He invades my space and grabs my hands. "We're fated. Don't you see that we're meant to be? There is no choice needed here. It's you and me, not you and Bellamy."

I jerk my hands away from him. "And that's the point of it all, isn't it? Choice. I didn't get a choice when Willow was murdered right in front of me. I didn't get a choice when Anders ripped me from my family. I didn't get a choice when Laik bit me. And when I finally did get to make a choice—to save you—you used that against me and then practically forced me to date your betas again. Now you're telling me that I don't have a choice in who I marry. You're wrong. I can choose to deny the fated bond if I want to. And I just might."

I turn and race back into the house, slamming the door behind me. I couldn't stay out there because, if I had, he'd have seen the tears. I sink onto the floor, entirely overcome with this decision. The sobs wrack my body painfully, like a punishment. It's true I have a choice here, but never before has it been so hard to make one. This choice will forever change my life.

If I choose Bellamy, there is no way we can stay here. Ryne proved last night that he will continue to fight for me, no matter what, and I won't put Bellamy through that.

And if I choose Ryne, is it really a choice at all?

CHAPTER 23

AFTER BREAKFAST, I gather the women I trust most: Madame Delphine, Elle, Joanna, and Faye. I need to talk about this, to get some solid advice. I realize I only have just over a month to make a decision, but I'm going to make sure it's mine.

We sit in Madame Delphine's office. Joanna is perched on the couch beside me with a pillow in her arms. She's been so quiet since she got back. She roomed by herself last night, and this is the first I've seen of her since, but she won't look at me. Not *really* look. It's like we don't even know each other anymore.

I lay it all out. I tell them just about everything that has happened with both Ryne and Bellamy and how I feel about them both. "And now I don't know what to do."

Faye snorts. "Why are you still denying it? Look at

what that man did for you. He risked his whole pack and his life. And you're still making him fight for it?"

Elle shakes her head. "I'm starting to go back to my original opinion on this one. Bellamy has been far better to you than Ryne has. He's such a good man too. Perfect, really. He'd never hurt you like Ryne has. If you love him, you should go with him."

I look at Joanna, but she's not exactly paying attention.

Madame Delphine clears her throat. "You still have one month, give or take a few days, so why not take that time to figure it out? Obviously, this is an unusual situation, and my choice would be Ryne, but you deserve to make this decision for yourself. Date them both. Go out with Ryne one night and Bellamy the next for the whole month. I would recommend not spending the night at either house as that could get out of hand quickly."

That's not a bad idea.

"I think I could do that. Do you think they'll be okay with it?"

"If they want a shot with you, they will be," Faye says.

Joanna shifts in her seat and shoots me a very serious expression. "I don't like any of this. I have no love for Ryne, but he is your fated, and I think he's right. You won't be able to deny it. So do Bellamy a favor, and when you realize that you want Ryne, don't drag it out any longer."

Elle shakes her head. "Or if you decide on Bellamy

early, then you should end things with Ryne once and for all."

I sit back, unsure of how to take this information.

The door crashes open, and we all jump. Ryne bursts into the room, face pale, and he's panting. When he sees Joanna, his eyes go wide.

Her hands fly up in surrender, and she jumps off the couch, her pillow flying across the room. "You were right about Laik, Grady was wrong, and I'm here because we must stop the lycans during the next full moon when they attack the villages again. Don't shoot the messenger."

"Where's Grady? Is he okay?"

"He's in hiding, but he's fine."

Ryne nods. "He's welcome back in my pack and as my beta. That's if he wants to come."

Joanna's mouth trembles. "Thank you."

"But we have bigger problems than the lycan," Ryne says, his eyes passing from each of us and finally landing on me. Fear clenches in my gut. Something is wrong. "The new alpha king has been chosen."

He sinks onto the couch Joanna just vacated. I can feel his heat from here and also his anxiety. A haunted look takes over his face.

"And who is it?" Madame Delphine asks carefully.

"Anders."

Of all the names he could've said, this one hurts the most.

Bile rises in my throat, and I clutch at my

abdomen. Panic sweeps through me, and so do the unwanted memories. They bombard me one after another, no matter how hard I wish them away. Anders groping my sister and then decapitating her for rejecting his advance. Anders taking me to the claiming in her place and then forcing me to date him, talking about marriage and sex, intimidating me into pretending I was okay with all of it. And then when we figured out that he killed Nova and Lexi, he turned everything around on us and convinced Thorn that Joanna and Grady were the problem. That they needed to die.

I hated Thorn. From the moment I met him, he made my skin crawl, and I'm not sorry he's dead.

But Anders? Anders is the true villain in my story.

I hate him with everything in me, with every breath, with every thought, with all of me—*I hate him.* But worst of all is the fear because, if I'm being honest with myself, I'm downright terrified of Anders. Even despite the gruesome lycan hiding under my skin, even despite the amazing friends at my side and the powerful shifters to protect me, I'm afraid. Nothing else matters because Anders will always be the one who hurt me the most. And the very thought of him as the alpha king and what that will mean for the future of this kingdom sends me into a tailspin.

He'll hurt my friends.

He'll kill Ryne.

And he'll rape me.

I sink to my knees, pressing my face into the rug as my vision blurs and my throat tightens.

"What the hell is wrong with her?" Faye squeals. I try to look up at her, but my neck won't move. Tears slip from my eyes.

I'm so hot. I'm shaking—and then Ryne is with me. Hand on my back. I can feel his calming presence, but I can't see him. I wish I could see him.

But all I can see is Anders and the terrible things he'll do now that he's king.

"She's having a panic attack."

I vaguely make out Madame Delphine's voice as the fear carries me into the dark.

I WAKE IN FAMILIAR ARMS. I blink rapidly and sit up as everything comes back to me. I'm in my room, and Ryne is lying with me on my small bed. He's asleep, despite the sun filtering through the curtains. And we're alone in here. How long was I out? I've never had something like that happen to me before, and my cheeks warm at the memory.

"Are you okay?" Ryne's eyes pop open and run over my body. "Are you thirsty? Do you need something to eat?"

I shush him. "Just tired. Looks like you're pretty tired yourself."

He tugs me back into his arms, his woodsy scent

enveloping me, calming me. I know I shouldn't, but I let him do it. I need the comfort I find there, even if it's only for a few minutes.

"Things are tense and busy," he mutters. "I haven't been sleeping well."

"Well, I'm glad you napped with me. How long was I out?"

"A few hours."

I shake my head. "I still can't believe it."

He squeezes my upper arm and pulls me in closer, brushing a kiss on my forehead. "You had a panic attack. Do you know what that is?"

I think about it for a moment, remembering an old neighbor who used to talk about those. It wasn't something my childhood brain needed to understand, so I never asked. "Vaguely."

"Everything that's happened is like someone piling rocks on your back. Eventually, you weren't going to be able to carry the weight anymore." He runs the tips of his fingers up my arm, leaving a trail of goosebumps. "I'm so sorry. It's all my fault."

My immediate reaction is to tell him that it's not his fault, but truthfully, a big part of it is. He's hurt me, abandoned me, and hasn't treated me the way I deserve. He's been one of the people piling those rocks up. And now with Bellamy, I know what it's like to have a man treat a woman well, to have someone take the rocks away.

I just wish I could love Bell the way I love Ryne.

I sit up again, scooting back on the bed to make some distance, and choose my words carefully. "I think we need to talk." He nods, brushing the hair from his face, and sits up too. "We have a lot of things to take care of before we worry about our relationship. First of all, Joanna needs our help. She has information on the next lycan attack, and if we're smart, we may be able to get rid of Laik and his cronies for good."

"She and I had a long conversation while you were asleep. Nico is already on his way to the panther pack to see if we can get their help. With the Carolina Pack being so vulnerable right now, we're going to need an ally, and since I've made the changes Derek wanted, I really think he might help us this time."

I nod, hopeful for the support but worried the panther leader will keep his neutral position.

"And then there's the matter of Anders."

His gaze turns murderous, blue eyes like thunder-clouds about to unleash lightning. "You let me worry about Anders."

What I'm about to say might come as a shock, but it needs to be said. "I know you don't want to leave the Carolina Pack, but you have to. Who else is going to stand up for the women all over the wolf kingdom? You're making a great start here, but if change is going to spread to the other packs, we need a good man as alpha king. Not Anders. He'll come here and put things back to the way your father had them or worse. The wolves that left have probably already told him what happened."

"Like I said, I'll take care of Anders." He stares at me for a long moment. "But I'm not making any moves against him right away, not when we're still adjusting to change here and have a vigilante group of lycans attacking our villages. If, in the end, we have to take the whole pack and move them out of Anders's reach, we will."

He's right. We have to worry about Laik right now. That's priority number one. Still, we can't run from Anders forever.

"But I really don't think Anders will show his face here anytime soon." He smirks. "He's always been afraid of me. He was only my number two because my father wanted a spy. I'm stronger than he is, and he knows it. And he also knows that I'll kill him if he tries to come here and take what's mine."

I sit back on my heels. "Okay, that's fair, but you need to accept the truth about yourself, Ryne. You're a hybrid now. Your wolf bite contains the lycanthrope virus and will kill any wolf shifter during the full moon. That's valuable. You could use that to kill Anders."

His face drains of color, and he's quiet for so long that I'm not sure he heard me. "I already know that," he finally whispers. "But you can't tell a soul, not even Bellamy or Elle or anyone else. If it gets out, I'll be hunted down and executed."

I frown, unable to believe that his most trusted

friends would hurt him. "Would they really do that to you?"

"Without a doubt." There's no hesitation in his voice. "If not my own pack, then certainly one of the other packs. And the more people who know, the more likely it is to get out. You and Callum are the only people who know about my bite. Callum has been a big help."

I nod because, even though I disagree that he needs to be so secretive, I understand. I have to hide my real self now too. We're the same in that, and it doesn't feel good, but it's better than the alternative. "Okay, and last thing . . . I still don't know how to forgive you for hurting me. I want to, and I'm grateful for all you're doing to help the claimed men and women, but I'm not sure I can trust you with my heart again."

"Poppy, please—"

"So I've decided that I'm going to date both you and Bellamy," I cut him off.

Heartbreak splinters across his face. I don't know if I've ever seen him so vulnerable, so hurt. The alpha is used to fighting for what he wants and getting it, but this time, he might not win, and he knows it. I recognize that with Anders being alpha king, I'm actually safer with Bellamy. Together, we can run away. Ryne can't. He has his whole pack to worry about. I will never be his number one priority.

"I have to be sure, and I'm just not there yet, so I would like to alternate dates between the two of you until the harvest festival. If I choose you, you'll get all of me, forever, and I'll never look back."

His eyes drift down to my mouth, and I have the sudden urge to kiss him. But I won't, not only because of the full moon coming up but because he needs to internalize what I'm about to say to him, to understand how serious I am with this decision. "But if I choose Bellamy, you must respect that. You can't hurt him, and you can't try to stop us if we get married and move to a new pack."

It's like we're frozen, staring at each other, the world going cold around us.

And then he moves so fast that I barely see it happen. One second, I'm sitting on the end of the bed, and the next, I'm flat on my back, and he's lying on top of me, caging me with his arms. He inhales deeply then drags his mouth from my temple to my jaw and down to my collarbone, peppering my skin with soft open kisses—but nothing else about him feels soft.

"Fine, we'll do it your way," he whispers against my ear, and my core burns hot, the frost gone in an instant. "But I'm going to give this little plan of yours my all, so you better prepare yourself, Poppy. Bellamy doesn't stand a chance. By the harvest moon, you won't even remember his name, but you'll be consumed with mine."

CHAPTER 24

I BOUNCE BACK and forth on both feet.

"Would you calm down?" Joanna presses a hand to my arm.

"Oh, come on, like you aren't just as excited."

We're standing on Ryne's porch, watching the road. Any second now, a car is going to pull up, and if all goes as planned, my family and Joanna's parents will be inside.

"I really wish we had another week," she says. "I'm not excited. I'm nervous."

"I know, but the full moon is tonight whether we like it or not."

The panther pack showed up early yesterday morning. Since half of Ryne's pack deserted him, there is plenty of room in the city. We spent a couple of hours going over a plan to take out Laik and his followers. First, we wanted to get everyone in a central location so they will be easier to protect. All the villagers will be transported into the city, and the wolves and panthers will guard it. Then, Ryne, Derek, me, Joanna, Grady, and a few others will go hunt down Laik. Any lycans who surrender will be restrained until the full moon is over and then allowed to go free. Ryne's wolves didn't like that idea, but Derek insisted that the lycans be protected if they didn't fight, and for once, I actually liked the guy.

My family is staying at Ryne's, and Joanna's parents are staying at Shauna's, but they're meeting us here. Women from all over the city are anxiously awaiting to see their relatives again. I wanted to go with the wolves to get them, but Ryne said it would be faster and easier if it was just the wolves since they could communicate with each other telepathically and because weepy reunions would slow things down.

He was probably right.

A car pulls up, and I straighten my skirt. Nerves dance in my stomach. "How do I look?"

Joanna laughs. "You look just as good as you did fifteen minutes ago when you asked. What about me?"

"Stunning as always." And she does. It's as if life was breathed back into her when Grady finally returned to the pack last night. He even got his old house back. Joanna's supposed to move in with him as soon as they're married, but I'm not sure she'll wait that long. Ryne won't care. He's just glad to have his old friend back. I'm unsure if Grady will ever truly forgive Ryne for the loss of his arm, but I hope they can become the brothers they once were.

Joanna grabs my hand, and we run for the car. Ryne climbs out first, and I wonder if he told my parents anything about our relationship. He extends a hand and helps my mother out of the car. She falls back a few inches when she sees me, her hand on her mouth. Ryne helps steady her, and I rush for her. She collapses into my arms, hugging me tighter than she ever has before. Another set of arms engulfs us, and I spot my dad out of the corner of my eye.

Then, two little arms wrap around my waist, and I nearly lose it. Mama pulls away, her hands on my cheeks. "I thought I'd never see you again."

I nod, sniffling, not sure what to say. It hasn't even been a year, but it feels like eons have passed.

"Poppy!" Evan squeals, and I pick him up.

He squirms. "I'm not a baby. Put me down."

I hold him close to me and kiss his cheek before setting him down. "We have food ready if you're hungry. You're staying here tonight. This is the alpha's house, so you know it's extra secure." I point up to the gorgeous house, and my mother's face pales.

"Aren't you staying with us?"

I shake my head. "No. I have to help protect the city." I won't tell her that I'm a lycan, not yet, but I can fight, and that's going to be my excuse.

"But you're just a girl. Is that what they brought you here for, to be warriors?"

Joanna, who'd been standing nearby with her parents, snorts. "Hardly. But we were taught to fight, and Poppy and I decided that we weren't going to sit back, defenseless. This is our home, our pack, and we will protect it."

My mom looks at Joanna suspiciously and takes Evan's hand. My dad hasn't said much, but he puts his arm around my shoulders. "We're so glad to be with you again. Ryne said, if we want, we can live in the city with you now."

It's hard to picture Papa living anywhere other than the farmland he loves, but the selfish part of me wants them to stay and make a life here.

"Yeah. You can."

"Do you live here?" he asks, marveling at the big home.

"If she wants to," Ryne says.

Evan looks from Ryne to me. "Is Ryne your boooyfriend?" he asks with a giggle.

Ryne plants a sloppy kiss on my cheek. "I am."

I push him away. I do not want to have that conversation right now. Evan creases his eyebrows. "I thought Knox was your boyfriend."

Everyone goes silent for a moment.

"Well, boyfriends can change," Mama says.

Evan shakes his head. "No way. Sarah is going to be my girlfriend forever. Can she live here too?"

Sarah is the little girl next door, and when I left, they couldn't stand each other. Willow and I used to tease him that they'd fall in love one day. Maybe we were right.

Before any of the rest of us say anything, Ryne adds, "Maybe. But not tonight. Tonight, everyone needs to stay where they are so they can be safe. We'll see about finding Sarah and her family tomorrow."

Sarah's older sister was claimed a few years ago. I hope they managed to find her tonight and are staying with her, but I'm not sure she's even alive.

"You all can go on inside. I have a few things to take care of. Poppy, I'll see you and Joanna in a couple of hours. I'll send someone to come and get you."

I watch him leave, then I lead my parents into his house.

"Ryne said that you could live here if you want, so where do you live now?" Mama asks.

"For the last year, I've lived in a home on the outskirts of the city with the rest of the claimed girls. I'll explain that all later. But for now, I want news from home."

The news turns out to be ordinary small-town things: couples getting married, breaking up, or having children. There's been a successful crop this year, but with all of us having to leave, it's unlikely all the available cotton will be harvested before it goes bad. I can tell that part bothers my father more than he lets on, but he doesn't say much about it.

"Oh, and a terrible flu swept through the village back in February. It nearly killed Old Man Lancaster, but he survived in the end. He always does." Mama adds, "Did you guys catch it here?"

I shake my head. "Wolves can't get sick, and not many humans are permitted to come and go from the wolf city, so I don't think we were ever exposed to it."

She nods thoughtfully. "Well, that's all going to change now."

I don't think lycan get sick either, but I don't mention it.

"I can hardly believe it," Papa sighs, his eyes going glossy, and I know he's thinking of Willow. I am too.

It's wonderful to be reunited with my family, but it's also a reminder of what we've lost, and that wound has been reopened now that we're together again. Or maybe it didn't heal for them, the same as it still hasn't for me. I'll never forget what happened to her, will never be okay with the brutality of her murder, but I hope the work we're doing now to make changes can help honor her memory. Because things are changing, just like Mama said. Papa may not believe it, but I do. I've fought way too hard to get to this point.

"Knock, knock," Bellamy says as he pushes open the front door. He's dressed in his best suit, and a little part of me stirs at the sight of him. His eyes go wide when he sees us all sitting in the front room, and then they soften, and he smiles. "You must be Poppy's family. You've raised a wonderful woman."

I jump to my feet, a blush forming on my cheeks. After I told Bellamy that I wanted to date both him and

Ryne leading up to the harvest, I expected him to be angry or hurt, but he wasn't. True to his personality, he was warm and understanding. But just like Ryne, he insisted he'd be the one to win me over in the end. He's so charming, so kind, so perfect—he just might.

"Who are you?" Evan asks. He shifts to stand in front of me with his legs spread and his arms crossed over his chest.

Joanna snorts. "That's your sister's *other* boyfriend."

I shoot her a death-glare, and she shrugs. "Hey, it wasn't my idea, remember?"

Papa appears a little confused, and my mother shoots me a look that I've only ever seen her give to a woman who cheated on her husband.

"Umm, well, you see, the thing is," I mumble. I've no idea how to explain all of this to them. It took me a few weeks to fully comprehend it all. This is such a different world from the one I was raised in.

"I'll explain," Bellamy says smoothly, shooting me a little wink and turning to my parents. "Dating multiple people is normal here. It's how we do things when a human woman is first brought into the city. She dates multiple shifter men and may even end up marrying one of them. I happen to be one of the two men Poppy is currently dating before she decides what she wants to do about a future spouse."

Mama and Papa nod, Joanna rolls her eyes, Evan frowns, and I just stand there, relieved. Mama's face still betrays her true feelings, but at least, she doesn't seem to feel the need to say anything. I'm glad he explained that so well because I obviously didn't know what to say. And I'm also glad that he didn't go into details about what else happens to the claimed women, although my parents might already know by now. If I were to explain to them what the claiming really meant, they'd be horrified. They'd hate the shifters, and who knows if they'd even stay here tonight. And I need them to stay because as long as they're safe, I won't be worrying about them while I'm off hunting down Laik.

"Okay, that's a good enough explanation for now," I insist. "Mama, Papa, Evan, this is Bellamy."

As soon as the introductions are complete, I'm ready to go, but Papa is already badgering Bellamy with questions. Where does he live? What does he do? Does he want children? I already know Bell's answers to the questions.

Papa leans back in his chair. "Do you date other women too?"

Bellamy shakes his head. "I'm required to, but it's not serious with anyone else. Not since I met Poppy. I'm really hoping she'll choose me over Ryne."

"What do you think of Ryne?"

That one shocks me, and I'll admit I'm curious to know the answer. "Ryne is a great alpha. I'm not sure if he'll be a great husband—I can't speak to that—but I will say he loves your daughter. Same as how I've fallen in love with her."

My cheeks flame, and his words shut everyone up,

me the most. Bellamy hasn't told me he loves me yet, and hearing him say those words to my father makes this all so real.

"Aw." Joanna breaks the silence. "Maybe I'm team Belly after all."

I raise my eyebrows at that because Joanna has been a strong proponent of the mating bond up until now, but when I catch her playful smirk, I know she's teasing me. I could kill her—now is really not the time.

"Team Belly?" Mama questions.

"You know, Bellamy plus Poppy equals Belly."

Evan laughs and pats his stomach. "Belly!"

"Alright, that's enough of that. We've really got to go," I interrupt, fighting back the embarrassment. Besides, I can already feel the moon calling to me even though it's hours until its light will be strong enough to turn me, and between that and everything else on my mind, I can't handle where this interrogation is headed. I give my parents one more hug each. Then I kneel in front of Evan and squeeze his hands with mine. "You stay safe tonight, okay? Promise to stay inside, and the wolves will protect you."

His eyes water. "And who will protect you?"

"I'll protect her," Bellamy says.

"We all will," Joanna adds. "We're going to look out for each other, okay? Same as you need to look out for your mom and dad."

He nods up at my friends, and I wrap him in a tight hug and leave before my family can see me cry. The truth is I don't know if Bellamy or Joanna or Ryne or Elle or *anyone* can protect me tonight. There's a pit in my stomach, one that's warning me things aren't going to be easy. Who knows how many lycans will be out there tonight attacking the villages? And of those lycans, how many will be going through their first transitions?

I shiver, just remembering how it felt to be so bloodthirsty, so unbelievably out of my mind that I was willing to feed on Knox. I would've killed him if they hadn't pulled me off. And Charlotte—she did kill during her first transition. She killed ruthlessly, without care, and would've taken out an entire basement of innocent women if given the chance. This virus makes us incredibly dangerous, and the newly turned lycans are the most dangerous of us all.

CHAPTER 25

THE ARMY of wolves and panthers protecting the city is pretty epic. They're everywhere—their coats shining bright in the dying sunlight, a mix of shaggy brown massive dogs and slick black powerful cats. I can hardly look away. If the lycans can see this now, they've got to be terrified. I would be. But knowing some of those lycans as I do, this sight is probably hyping them up.

More blood for them to spill.

Ryne had scouts out all day, who discovered that Laik and his people have mostly gathered near a fishing village. It's one of the farthest from the city, splitting us from the bulk of the army if we decide to go to them instead of waiting for them to come to us. It makes me uneasy, and I'm not sure what Laik is playing at. He obviously changed his plan to attack the textile village, which is much closer and honestly made more sense. He must know we've taken all the humans into the city, so then why gather his troops so far away?

We're standing on the dock preparing to leave for battle, and I turn back to gaze at the betas' homes and the high-rise buildings in the distance. At least, the main ways into the city are by boat or bridge. The bridge is so heavily guarded that there's no way the enemy could cross it. The backroads are all being guarded too, as is the shoreline. The entire territory is crawling with wolves and panthers, but that won't stop Laik from trying to take us down. I hope the defenses hold because I won't be there to protect those inside the city if it falls, and it makes me sick just thinking about it.

"It's not too late to stay back. You're going to get hurt," Grady pleads with Joanna.

She widens her stance. "No way. We've been over this before. Where you go, I go. I've got two swords and knives hidden on my body. I'm going to fight with you."

I don't want Joanna to come either. It's so risky. The most vulnerable people need to be behind the army for protection, not out in front of it, and she's going to be target number one since she betrayed Laik.

"But what if you get bitten by a lycan?" His voice sounds as haunted as I feel.

"Poppy and Ryne worked it out. We can too."

"You know that's not totally true," I interject, tired of their argument. Joanna is being foolish, but she has a right to make her own choices. "I was lucky to survive the bite. Not everybody does. *And* I could still end up with Bellamy." We're leaving him at the bridge as he's in charge of the wolves guarding it. He was just here to give me a big hug and a kiss on the cheek and made me promise to be safe, and Ryne is already acting icy about it.

"You and Bellamy are only dating because Ryne messed up," Joanna points out. "It's not because you're a lycan."

Ryne shoots her a scathing look, but she only rolls her eyes.

I give her a hard glare. "There's a good chance you're not walking away from tonight still a human. Is that what you want?"

"See," Grady implores. "Poppy gets it."

Joanna holds up a hand. "That's enough, you two. I've made up my mind."

"Are you ready for this?" Derek asks gently, untying the boat from the dock. I nod, and he takes my hand, helping me climb aboard. I don't let myself think too hard as the rest of the boat fills, and Ryne starts the engine.

We take it to the inlet near the fishing village and hide it in the endless marshes that filter the rivers from the sea. From here, it's only another mile on foot, and as we near the village, Joanna and Grady start bickering about her coming along again. I smile because it's great to have them back even if the reunion between Grady and the pack was less than welcoming. Ryne was ecstatic, but everyone else? Not so much. It's going to take time to heal those wounds, but I'm confident Ryne will make sure they do heal.

After a while of hiking, Ryne steps up between us, and we all stop. He looks up at the sky. It's clear tonight, not a cloud in sight, and the sunset has cast everything in wild shades of orange. "Quit arguing, you two," he shoots at the couple. "She's here, the moon's almost up, and it's nearly go time."

"Remember, he is our goal," Derek instructs his number two, a quiet man named Ace. I can't help but wonder if Ace is his real name or his nickname.

Ace nods, and Ryne continues, "We avoid fights with any and all of the others unless it's self-defense. Once Laik is dead, I will try to persuade them to stop."

A few minutes later, we find a stand of trees just outside the village that makes for a good hiding spot. From here, we can see people prowling around, but we're too far away to make out their faces. I wonder if I know any of them. Ryne emptied the village already, so they're definitely all lycan. The last rays of sun dip behind the trees, the full moon taking center stage.

My bones crack.

"Here we go," I say, hurrying to slip from my human clothing. Callum and the shifters do the same.

This transition is even easier than the last, and my mind is totally clear within seconds.

"See," Joanna whispers. "Look how badass she looks. I could totally do that."

Grady shakes his head and growls. "You stay with me, and don't even think about letting yourself get bit."

Ryne, Derek, Ace, and Grady all shift. Joanna scrambles onto Grady's back. We discovered earlier that Ryne and Derek can communicate in their shifted forms, so they'll be able to relay messages back and forth between the packs. But it's an alpha thing only, so if one of them is killed, our plan could dissolve into chaos.

I allow my mind to relax so I can hear what's going on with the lycans. I thought it would be difficult to find Laik, but apparently, he doesn't think we'd be listening because in moments, he's broadcasting to all the lycan. *The wolves have taken all humans into their city . . .*

Poppy, are you ready? Ryne interrupts the thoughts from Laik.

I am, I reply so only Ryne can hear me.

I will be going into the village first since I'm a lycan, and unless I come across someone who knew me well from the wilds, no one else will recognize me or think anything of me moving among them. Callum is going to stay with Ryne and the others. Once I find Laik, I'll notify the others where I am, and only then will we reveal ourselves to him and fight.

I prowl through the village, which is much larger than mine. Rounding a corner, I nearly falter when I catch sight of the glittering ocean. I've never seen the ocean before, only heard stories. It's an endless stretch of rolling water leading into nothing but inky black. An old lighthouse stands vigil over everything on a cropping of rocks farther out. The smell of salt and fish permeates everything, heightened by my lycan senses.

Several lycans take off toward the wolf city. On foot, it would take a human three hours, but the lycans are incredibly fast, and I know they'll be there in one. It's difficult for me not to want to try and stop them. My family is in the city, and I want to protect them, but taking out Laik is our primary goal, so I don't. I trust that the wolves and panthers guarding the city will do their jobs.

I follow Laik's voice. I'm pretty sure he's stationary, and I wonder why he's not going into the city with the rest of them. Maybe he's letting them fight first so he doesn't risk his own life.

Coward.

I turn a corner and then back up. He's there with a dozen other lycan, all of whom look like they are waiting for something, though what exactly that is, I don't know.

Steadying myself, I peek around the corner. I recognize Laik's and Wanda's lycan forms, but not the others. Aside from Wanda, they are all very big and bulky, so they're probably male. Laik stands in the middle of them, and when Wanda darts off into the village, I become uneasy.

I send the location back to Ryne. *Something is off, though. It's like he's waiting for us. This could be a bloodbath. He's got too many guards.*

We're better than they are. We can beat them.

I want to argue, but I know Ryne. He's already on his way. *See you soon.*

I stay hidden while I wait. And wait. No reason to make myself known and ruin any chance we have at a surprise, but I'm growing impatient. I can hear them rustling around. Maybe I should move a little farther away. I'm not that well hidden.

Suddenly, a lycan jumps in front of me, and I glance up to meet his cruel eyes.

Laik.

Hello, Poppy. We've been waiting for you.

CHAPTER 26

SURRENDER NOW, *Laik,* I demand. But really, I'm trying to buy myself time. Laik isn't the type to surrender under any circumstance. Not now. Not ever. And I'm not the type to take such a horrible person prisoner when he deserves death.

His laugh penetrates my mind. *Why would I surrender when I've already won?*

There's not enough of you to take down the wolf pack, I say, *even if you've bitten a bunch of humans, there still won't be enough to stop us. You're just going to get innocent people killed.*

I might die, but we're going to win.

We have to.

I don't want to reveal that we've got panthers on our side yet—that our numbers have grown exponentially for this battle. He'll find out soon enough if he doesn't already know.

Because of the panthers? He guesses, stalking in close as several other lycan appear behind him. They've backed me into a corner, and if they wanted to kill me now, there's enough of them that they could. I will Ryne and the others to hurry. I can feel it all the way to my bones—my time is short. He bares his teeth. *Oh, we know all about those traitors. In fact, we've already taken Derek out.*

I stare at his grotesque lycan form silhouetted in the moonlight, unwilling to accept what he just said. I just saw him minutes ago. How could he be dead already? Ryne and Grady were with him. If he's dead, then so are they.

My heart sinks.

That's not possible. The words slip through the telepathic bond without me even realizing, and he laughs again.

Turns out, not every panther is as soft and pathetic as their leader. I already got confirmation from Wanda that our panther on the inside took him out. I believe you've met Ace already? My mate was there to see it happen.

Ace is a traitor? Oh no. No, no, no. A horrible vision of Wanda tearing through Ryne's house and finding my family flashes through my mind. She won't even hesitate—she'll kill them, and she'll like it. If I don't stop this, I have no doubt she'll be on her way to the wolf city soon.

Now stand back, Laik says to his lackeys. *I've been waiting for this moment.*

And then he attacks.

I duck as his body comes barreling toward me. I swing up on his other side and jump onto the roof of the nearby structure then take off running. I can't fight him when he's got backup, and I don't. I need to give my team more time to get to me.

I'm running toward the lighthouse, I tell Ryne, hoping he's still alive to hear me. *I've got Laik chasing me. Meet me there?*

Already on the way. I can hear his strained voice, the worry that wasn't there minutes ago. But it's nothing compared to the relief I feel that he's still alive.

Do you already know about Derek?

He's dead. Ace turned on us. Grady was quick, though. He killed Ace after it happened.

Quick. But not quick enough.

What does this mean for the panther pack?

Careful, I add. *Wanda will be on your tail.*

In all of two minutes, I've bounded from the rooftops to the beach and over to the rocky coastline where the aging lighthouse waits. Up close, I can tell that the thing is half-crumbling and about ready to topple over.

You want me? Come get me! I call out to everyone in the vicinity and sprint toward the lighthouse, tearing the door clear off its rusty hinges and climbing the old spiraling staircase. The metal groans under my weight.

I'm going to enjoy this, Laik sneers. He's only a few yards behind me, his claws outstretched and teeth gleaming. He's bigger than I am and gaining ground, and my muscles burn as I push myself to the very top of the lighthouse. There's a large broken light inside a dome and a circular walkway around the whole thing. We're completely exposed to the elements. There's nowhere else to go.

I've got you now, Poppy. You're dead.

We circle the broken light, and I edge to the railing, the cold wind whipping against my face. I'm taller in this form, which makes the height seem even worse. I can't believe I thought coming up here was a good idea. Laik pounces, and I quickly dodge him, but then I slip, grabbing onto the edge of the railing. It bends, and then I'm swinging, dangling off the edge.

He crouches low. *It's a long fall down, and those rocks look sharp, don't they?*

No, please don't. My voice quivers as my claws begin to slide. One slips free, and then I'm hanging by only a few claws and nothing else. I'm about to die.

I'm so glad I got to hear you beg before I killed you, Laik taunts.

And then he slams down on my paw, and I can't help it—I let go.

I never imagined this would be how I would die. I didn't actually think about death all that much until this last year when I started to think about it constantly. I would be torn apart by lycans or wolves. I would be murdered by someone like Anders, strangled or drowned or beaten to death. Maybe one of the other claimed women would poison me. Or maybe I'd die of a broken heart. There were so many possibilities. But falling?

And I do fall. It's fast and horrifying.

But when I land, pain doesn't explode through my body.

Because another lycan has caught me. I blink up into his face, trying to place him, but my vision is blurred, and my heart is pounding.

Are you okay? Knox's voice asks.

I nod, stunned.

Oh, thank goodness, Charlotte adds over his shoulder.

Knox sets me down, and we step back as several other lycans surround us. *Traitors,* one of them calls to the others. *Knox and Charlotte are traitors.*

You're the traitors, Knox spits. *You know the changes that have been made to the Carolina Pack, and you still want to kill them all in cold blood.*

I'm thrilled to see my friends have returned to me, but a murderous growl sounds from above, distracting everyone. Laik still stands up there, but he's not alone. Ryne's black wolf circles him, his growl darker and more threatening than ever before. In moments, the two predators are on each other, snarling and howling. We lose them from view for a second, and my heart races all over again. If Ryne dies, I don't know what we'll do.

All the lycans scramble back to get a better view of

the fight, but some break away from the group to charge toward the lighthouse.

However, they're met with Callum, the wolves, and Joanna.

She really is covered in knives.

"Try me," she hisses through gritted teeth, holding up two long knives. "I'd love some target practice."

One of the lycan pounces, and she throws the knife so fast he doesn't see it coming. It slices straight through his neck, and the creature slumps to the ground.

"Who's next?" she asks, and Grady growls at her side.

Nobody moves.

Then a lycan breaks free and manages to make it through the door, dodging our people and all of Joanna's knives. I recognize her at once.

Wanda.

I race back up the stairs after her. We make it to the top and see Ryne and Laik locked in battle. Wanda leaps, but I'm on top of her before she can reach them. Her body cracks the wall of bricks, and when she fights to flip over, I make sure we turn into the lighthouse so I don't go flying off the edge again. She's all teeth and claws, and it's all I can do to keep her from tearing my neck out. My back is to the glass of the lighthouse. It's weak, but it's holding. I manage to get a leg up, and I shove with all my might, and her body goes flying right off the edge.

At the same time, I hear a loud snarling sound, and another body flies through the air.

I glance over and see Ryne peering down to where both bodies landed, torn up by rocks.

Laik and Wanda are dead.

CHAPTER 27

I TURN to head back down the stairs, but Ryne stops me.

We need to get our stories straight, he says.

What do you mean? We're moving fast. There's not a lot of time to come up with a story, and I'm not even sure we need to.

Well, I don't know how the hierarchy works for the lycans, but if it's similar to the way things work for wolves, then whoever killed Laik will be the next alpha.

But they don't have to listen to their alpha, I reason. *They choose an alpha. It's not like with you shifters.*

Exactly. They won't know which one of us killed him, so you should assert yourself as alpha.

Excuse me? This wasn't the plan.

You're more than capable of leading them. His wolf form is majestic, and all I can think is that he's the one who people will want to follow, not me. Never me.

If I try to bring lycans into my pack, he continues, *my wolves might revolt. This way, we can still have some semblance of peace.*

The last thing I want is for the wolves to revolt, but the thought of outing myself is terrifying. *Very few people know I'm a lycan. Wouldn't it be too dangerous? You said yourself there are wolves who would kill you if they found out you were a hybrid, and I'm the full thing.*

His voice comes through our link, rough and determined. *You're right. And that's why we're not going to let everyone know your true identity. For now, I'm going to head back to the city, corral the panthers and my men, and you're going to get the lycans under control. You can do this, Poppy. I know you can. I believe in you.*

But I don't believe in myself—I'm not meant for leadership.

It's a good idea, though. And as long as I make it through the night, Ryne and I can figure out the details later. And if I can convince the other lycans to call off the attack, so many lives will be spared.

Silence surrounds us once we hit the bottom of the stairs. There are so many more lycans than there were before, and everyone has gathered around the bodies, just staring.

No one is fighting.

No one seems to know exactly what to do now.

One of the lycan turns and spots us. He nudges the one next to him, and soon they're all turning to face us.

The wolf killed our alpha. He dies now.

As the lycans descend on us, I step in front of Ryne. *No. I killed your alpha. That means you answer to me.*

They all stop, the few in front breathing hard. I recognize a few of them from Laik's pack. I wonder if they recognize me.

We don't have to listen to you, Poppy, the one in front says, and my insides squeeze. The lycans knowing me is one thing, but what if they are able to somehow tell the wolves? Things just got so much more complicated. But then Callum, Charlotte, and Knox step up next to me, and I feel like maybe I'll be okay.

We have an alpha so that we can be organized like the wolves and not descend into chaos, Callum says. *She killed Laik. She's the new alpha of this pack. If you don't like it, you can leave. But if you try to hurt anyone in the city or surrounding villages, we will kill you.*

No one moves for a moment. Then something unexpected happens. The lycan in front drops to his knees and bows his head like I'm some sort of queen.

Then slowly, the others follow suit, including Callum, Charlotte, and Knox.

You know, my wolves don't even bow to me, Ryne says so only I can hear, and I catch the laughter in his voice. If I was human right now, no doubt, I'd be bright red.

Get out of here while you can. I'll see what I can do about stopping the others on their way to the city.

Ryne leaves with Grady, Joanna, and the other wolves, and I plan to wait until they are out of sight before I address the lycans again. I wonder if Ryne will hear my projection. I'm still not sure how to open communication to him and the others at the same time. I nudge Callum and Knox, who are on either side of me, and they stand. There are a couple hundred lycans on the beach by now, way more than I've ever seen gathered together before. I don't know how many more are heading into the city, but I pray they hear what I have to say—for all our sakes.

Who was Laik's second in command?

The lycan in front of me stands as well. *Wanda. After her, it was me.*

What's your name? I ask, but his voice is vaguely familiar.

Christian. You know me.

And I do. He was one of the people I spent those three months with. I didn't particularly care for him, but I didn't hate him either.

What was the plan tonight? I ask.

He sent all the new lycans into the city and kept the experienced ones out here. We were going to go in after the initial bloodbath.

I can picture it now, the screams and chaos and death. We're not out of the woods yet. Those new lycans are going to be thirsty, no matter who is the alpha. *How many were there?* I ask.

About fifty. Maybe more.

I project my voice to all the lycans I possibly can, not knowing how far it will travel. At least I know these ones will follow me. *I do not agree with Laik's plan to turn innocent humans into lycan to build an army, and I'm sorry if you were bitten against your will. I know how that feels as the previous alpha did the same thing to me. But he's dead, and as your new alpha, I want you to understand that biting innocent humans against their will is not tolerated.* A few lycan shift uneasily, but nobody argues, so I continue. *Prince Ryne and the Carolina Pack are not our enemy. They are working to make changes to their system for the betterment of all species. The time will come when you will likely have to fight wolves again, but not tonight, and not this pack.*

The lycans near me agree. I can feel their support.

This might work . . .

Thoughts from the new lycans bombard my mind from all angles, harsh bits of their cruel bloodlust. They're not going to heed me—they're already set on their course. And the worst part is I can't blame them. I know what it feels like to be going through your first renewal, to be dying for flesh, to be willing to do anything to get that first taste. And the second and the third.

We have to stop them, even if it means killing them, and maybe this decision is what it means to be an alpha. Protect the many even at the cost of the one.

Tonight, we will protect the humans and shifters from the newborn lycans. We are to go into the city and bring any lycan who cannot control themselves out. We will get hurt, and if we must kill to protect ourselves or others, then that's what we'll do. We will not attack a wolf or panther unless in self-defense. Any questions?

What if we don't agree with you? someone calls out.

Then you may leave. The woods are that way. I point away from the city.

I expect a few to leave, maybe even most. But none do.

I turn and run toward the city, my new pack following close behind.

I SLEEP until noon the next day. It's not enough sleep, but it'll have to do. I have people to see and plans to sort out. Ryne convinced the wolves and panthers to not attack the lycan before we arrived, and together, we were able to protect all the humans. As far as I could tell, no one was bitten, and aside from Derek, Ace, Laik, and Wanda, no one else died. Once the lycans shifted back, most of them left with the panthers for The Sanctuary, but a few decided to stay. Ryne's ordered nobody to touch them, but I fear that won't hold up against prejudices that run deep.

I collapsed into bed as soon as daybreak hit.

"You reek." Faye shakes me awake.

I blink at her. "I know. Hazard of the job."

"Take a shower before coming into *our* room next

time," she huffs. "Anyway, Madame Delphine asked me to give you this."

I look at the paper in her hand. It's a calendar.

"Thirty days until the harvest moon," she says. "It's the dating schedule."

I roll my eyes. "All the changes we've gone through, and the claiming is still happening."

Faye shrugs. "Some of us like it. And it's not like those who don't get chosen are going to the mating houses. And we all can say no if we want to. But you know I want Justin, and I'm pretty sure Lev is angling for Marissa. If you don't end up with Bellamy, I think he'll drop out."

I glance at the calendar. I'm on dates every night, alternating between Bellamy and Ryne, as expected. Elle is actually with Bell or Ryne on all of the nights I'm not, and nobody else gets any dates with Ryne. Just then, Elle bursts into the room, waving another copy of that stupid calendar around.

"You're welcome," she says, beaming at me.

"For what?"

"For not allowing lunas to go after your men. This dating schedule is a waste of time for most of us, but Madame Delphine is insistent upon it, so I convinced her to just let you and me date your guys. We all know Bell's not interested in anyone but you, and I'm never going to be Ryne's sloppy seconds, so I'm no threat."

I laugh and slide out of bed. "Who says you're not going to try to steal one of them?"

She wiggles her eyebrows. "You never know, do you?"

Faye gapes at her. "How did you manage that? I still have to share Justin."

"I asked." She bats her eyelashes. "That and I'm Madame Delphine's favorite."

Faye shoves her out of the way and storms down the hall.

"And you're her favorite too, you know." Elle wrinkles her nose. "You need to shower."

"So I've been told."

After I shifted back into my human body early this morning, I went over to Ryne's to make sure my family was okay. Dad was awake and sitting on the porch steps as if waiting for me. He didn't ask about what happened —he just patted me on the back and told me that they'd already decided to head back home. They have no interest in moving to the city, and while I wasn't surprised, I was a little disappointed. Once things are settled here, I'm going to visit home for a few weeks. Of course, we spent a few hours catching up before they left, but there's no denying that things are different than they used to be. Our family has been through trauma, and we just aren't bonded in the same way anymore. I hope we can repair things later because right now I have to stay in the city.

At least, I'm with Ryne tonight, which is good because we have a ton to discuss. We need to figure out what the next steps are, how we're going to keep my lycan identity a secret, and what to do about Anders. There's so much going on that dating seems almost comical at this point. Being an alpha is harder than I thought it was, and now that I'm alpha to the Carolina Pack's enemy, I'm afraid our future is more doomed than ever.

CHAPTER 28

THE TIGHT FLOOR-LENGTH gown wraps around my body like a second skin, accentuating my small curves. Ryne had delivered it to me earlier, and when I pulled it out of its velvet box, I gasped. I've never loved a dress so much. It's black as midnight with sparkling blue thread woven throughout like starlight. As I stare at it in the mirror, I can't stop thinking about the way the blue reminds me of Ryne's eyes. It's stunning. I love it, and I look great in it, but I don't know why I need to dress so extravagantly for a date the night after such a big event. I'm still processing everything, and I plan to use this time with Ryne to strategize.

"He's here," Faye says, popping her head into our room. "Go get your man."

I roll my eyes but head down to him, suddenly nervous.

He meets me at the door, his step faltering and his

breath catching when he sees me. "You look stunning," he whispers, and those cobalt eyes are bright as he stares at me, taking me in. He has no shame, his eyes admiring every curve. It sends a flutter of longing through me.

"You planned this." I motion to his perfectly tailored blue suit, the same color as the sparkles in my dress.

"We're fated mates. It's only right that we match."

My lips quirk into a smile, and he leads me out to the car, opening my door. There's no driver today. It's just us. When he slides into the driver's seat, I'm the first to speak.

"Have you heard anything from the panther pack yet?" They're going to have to pick a new alpha, and we're not sure what that's going to mean for The Sanctuary.

Ryne squeezes my hand, threading our fingers together. He brings our clasped hand up to his mouth and drops a soft kiss on my knuckles. "After a period of mourning, they will vote on their leadership. It's not like here. Don't worry. The panthers overwhelmingly support The Sanctuary, so whoever the alpha ends up being, we can count on them."

I release a breath. "Okay, and what about the lycans who stayed here? You really think they're not going to be hunted down and killed?"

His eyes flash. "Not on my watch. . . . Poppy, I want this date to be like any other normal date between a man and a woman, not like two alphas in the middle of a war. Can you do that for me? Can we not talk about anything related to the war and our roles in it?"

I frown, immediately anxious. "But there's so much to discuss." And really, this whole dating thing seems silly. We've got things to do and people to protect.

"And we will discuss everything tomorrow. Tonight, it's just about Poppy and Ryne."

"Poppy and Ryne," I repeat, my voice wobbly. "Okay, I can do that." But I'm not sure I can. Ryne and I have been through so much, and yet, my soul yearns for him.

He smiles, truly smiles. And when Ryne smiles, the whole world turns golden.

We drive to the downtown area. I'm a little uneasy because this is where most of the mating and pack houses are located. I haven't been down here since he announced the changes. But I don't say anything as Ryne leads me to the tallest building, and we slip into the elevator.

He pushes the button for the highest floor, and then as we're riding up, the inertia tugs at my belly. He cages me in the corner of the small elevator. His mouth hovers near my ear, his scent surrounds me, and my heart speeds. I think he's going to whisper something in my ear, but he growls instead and kisses my neck. And that's even better. If I focus on the way he makes me feel physically, then I don't have to think about the things we need to talk about. Not just the problems in our world but the problems that happened between us.

The doors open, and he steps back. "This way."

There's a metal door at the end of the hallway, and he opens it to a set of stairs. Up we go, right up to a flat rooftop. A small round table is set up with dinner, and soft music plays on the wind.

"Some say this is the best view in the city," he brags.

I step forward to take it all in, my mouth popping open at the blanket of city lights. Just like the stars, they sparkle. And just like my dress, they remind me of my mate.

"I would have to agree with that statement."

He studies me, his eyes brimming with so many emotions, so much love and grief and passion and hope, that it's impossible to look away. "I've always loved this view," he confesses, "but it's so much more beautiful with you in it."

I step forward and play with his suit jacket, thinking. If Bellamy weren't in the picture, would I be hesitating at all? Or would I have moved into Ryne's house? He hurt me. A lot. But he also came back to me. And the truth is my heart never really left.

"What's on your mind?" he prods gently.

I fiddle with his shirt, my fingers grazing over the buttons. "I don't know. You said you wanted this to be about Poppy and Ryne, and I'm so glad it is. I desperately want to move past the hurt and pain we have between us. I want to forget that you deserted me when I needed you most."

Ryne stiffens. "Poppy, I'm trying so hard here. What

else can I do to prove my love? I've done everything you've asked. And I've given you space to explore things with Bellamy—something that takes a lot more self-control than you think. I know I've messed up. I'm truly sorry, but I was scared. I didn't want you anywhere near me if I was about to be overthrown by my own pack, and I was angry that I wasn't strong enough to beat my father myself. I never should've pushed you away like I did, and I want to spend the rest of my life making it up to you."

He places a finger on my chin and lifts my face so I'm looking into his eyes. They search mine, pleading for forgiveness, and something inside of me snaps. All the hurt and pain disappears. I love this man. Deeply. I want nothing more than to be his forever.

I close the distance between us, pressing my lips against his, and he tugs me closer, deepening the kiss. So much pain is washed away in that kiss. I feel the tears slipping down my cheeks, relief and sorrow mingled together.

Ryne pulls back and wipes the tears away. "What's the matter?"

I shake my head, unable to speak.

He places light kisses on my cheeks. "I love you, Poppy."

"I love you too." My voice cracks. I'm so overcome by this man, by this love.

It's all-consuming.

He gives me a crooked grin. "Look at that. It's the

night after the full moon, you kissed me, and I'm still standing."

"Maybe that bite was good for something after all."

"Maybe it was."

He takes my hand and leads me over to the table. We eat and talk and laugh. It's the most relaxed I've ever been with him, and it takes every ounce of will not to go home with him that night.

I make him take me back to Drayton Hall, where I lie in bed for a long time, wondering if I've just made my choice, but I'll never know if I don't see Bellamy too.

Yet, I find that I don't want to.

I want Ryne and only Ryne.

THE NEXT THREE weeks pass in a blur. I continue dates with both Bellamy and Ryne, but Bellamy seems to be falling further and further away from my heart, and I think he knows it.

I arrive home early in the morning from an overnight date with Bellamy. He took me out to the panther city to visit with the few lycans who know I'm their alpha. It wasn't terribly romantic, and we didn't share a bed, but it was necessary, and I appreciated his willingness to take me.

He walks me to the front door. I lean up and give him a kiss on the cheek. "Thanks for that. It was fun."

He chuckles. "Fun is not a word I'd use to describe

it. But it was productive. Ryne asked me to take you out there and do some recon while I was at it."

I cock my head. I hadn't realized that.

"He did? I didn't realize you and he were so close." In fact, Ryne won't even speak his name around me anymore. When we're together on our dates, it's just us. Every time.

"Ryne made me his second."

I hadn't seen that coming, and I don't know how I missed it. Well, yes, I do. It's because I'm too busy with all the other things on my mind.

"I did not know that. Congratulations. Though, I do wonder what Ryne is thinking. That gives you even more incentive to want him dead. If something happens to him, you get me, and you become acting alpha."

"We talked about that, actually. But he recognizes that I've been working with getting the women out of the mating houses for far longer than he has, and so I'm less likely to rebel against him than anyone else now that he's doing the right thing."

"That makes sense." It still makes me uneasy. I trust Bellamy—I do—but so much has happened that it's hard not to be worried.

He slips his hands into his pockets and looks at me, his eyes searching mine. "Poppy, have you made your decision?"

My insides go cold, and I swallow. I don't want to talk about this; I'm too much of a coward to break his heart. I fiddle with my hair. "I have another week before I have to do that."

"I know. But I'm just asking. If you've made up your mind, then why bother keeping up this charade?"

"I . . . I . . . don't know."

He steps forward, trapping me between his body and the front door. He places both hands on either side of me.

"You know I would make you happy. You would always be my first priority."

I nod but don't say anything. Now that I'm an alpha myself, I understand Ryne so much better. I would do just about anything to make sure my pack is protected, even at the expense of my own interests, and maybe even my own heart.

Bell's lips press to mine, full of hunger and need and want. A month ago, I would've melted into this kiss. But today, it feels wrong. Broken. A mere shadow compared to the real thing.

He pulls away, and the tortured look in those green eyes says it all.

"That's what I thought. Goodbye, Poppy."

I trudge up the stairs, both relieved and a little sad. Though, my stomach buzzes at the thought of what Ryne's going to say when I tell him. I doubt I'll be spending the night in my own room tonight. I should probably get some sleep today.

I push open the door and find Elle sitting on my bed. She's fiddling with a pillow.

"You had a date with Bellamy last night."

I nod. "Yeah. You have fun with Ryne?"

She rolls her eyes. "By fun, you mean listening to him whine about you all night? No way."

I chuckle and sit down next to her, resting my head on her shoulder. Suddenly, I'm exhausted.

"You spent the night with Bellamy." Her voice is stiff and angry. It's new for her—Elle is one of the most level-headed people I've ever met. Even with the loss of her father, she's been so strong.

"Not really. He took me out to the panther sanctuary to meet with a few of the lycan. It was a long drive. Mostly, we were with other people all night, and we didn't share a bed."

She relaxes next to me. "Oh. I see."

I want to tell her about my decision. The one I hadn't even realized I'd made. But Ryne deserves to hear it first.

"I need some sleep," I yawn.

"You're going to break one of their hearts."

I swallow. "We've been over this before. They both knew the risks, and so did I."

She slides off the bed. "Whatever. Get some sleep. I'll see you later."

I slip under the covers and wonder why she's suddenly cold and angry with me, but I don't have the energy to deal with it. Instead, I let my eyes close, dreaming of the night to come.

CHAPTER 29

EVERY DATE with Ryne is special, but this one is going to be unforgettable, and I can't keep the grin off my face all afternoon as Joanna helps me get ready. She still has her own room in the manor, but she's with Grady most of the time, and I rarely get to see her, so it's nice to have her for the afternoon.

"How dare you?" Faye's shrill voice comes from the library, and we run out to see what's going on.

She's standing head-to-head with Violet and Cecily. Violet has a triumphant smirk on her face, and Cecily twirls her long blonde hair. They're both dressed up for their dates tonight with Lev and Justin, looking as beautiful as ever, but that's nothing new.

Violet pops her hip and folds her arms over her ample cleavage. "We have as much right to date the betas as you do."

"Actually, we have more of a right," Cecily adds. "We're lunas."

"What's going on?" Joanna asks, and I set my hand on Faye's shoulder to let her know we're here for her. It's not like the lunas haven't gone on dates with betas before, including Justin.

"Oh, Faye's just feeling insecure because Justin kissed Cecily on their last date," Violet says, her eyes shooting to Faye. "And I'm sure he will again on their date tonight."

"That's not what happened." Faye clenches her fists and glares at Cecily, who stands there with her chest out and a winning smirk on her painted lips. "He came to me today saying that you kissed him, and he stopped it. And now you're trying to make me think he cheated on me, but I know that's a lie."

"They just want to come between you," I say. "Don't listen to them."

"Oh, really? Maybe she deserves to know the truth so she isn't surprised when Justin chooses someone else next week," Violet interjects.

"That's if I'll even have him." Cecily yawns playfully. "I'm not sure he's my type, and he wasn't that great of a kisser."

I have to fight not to roll my eyes.

"That's funny, considering he probably had to push you off of him," Joanna says.

"Have you ever considered that we're not the enemy

here?" Violet's words drip with toxicity as she glares at us. "You humans know nothing. Second to fated mates, wolves are drawn to lunas. That's just the way it is. If they can have one of us, they're going to take that opportunity. Justin may say he loves Faye, but he's playing her."

"You're a liar!" Faye jumps on Violet, and both lunas immediately shift, their dresses ripping free and their white wolves growling up at us. If we don't get away, they might rip us to shreds before the house mothers arrive. I drag Joanna and Faye to our room before they get themselves killed.

Faye wipes tears from her eyes, and her face is nearly as auburn as her hair. "What if they're telling the truth?"

I hug her, and the three of us sit on her bed.

"I don't believe they are, but even if Justin does betray you, you're going to be okay," Joanna says, and I'm proud of my friend for forgiving Faye since she's returned. I know it wasn't easy.

"But I love him." Faye's voice cracks. "And he's the only man who's ever loved me back. Sure, I've had lots of attention from men for years..." Faye wrings her hands, and Joanna rolls her eyes behind Faye's back. "But they never saw the real me. And then Justin did."

"And he still does." I squeeze her hand. "And you know what? So do I."

She scoffs at that.

"It's true. You're one of my best friends, which is

saying something considering that we used to hate each other."

"Yeah," she sighs. "I was a mean bitch, but I've changed, you know?"

"I do know, but guess what? You're still one of the strongest people I've ever met, and if Justin breaks your heart, you're going to heal and be stronger than ever. It's just in your nature."

"She's right, you know," Joanna agrees. "You're a mean bitch for a reason."

Faye laughs and nods once. "You're right. If he's stupid enough to choose one of those stuck-up lunas over me, then that's his loss, not mine."

"What will you do?" Joanna asks, and I want to elbow her in the ribs for that, but Faye doesn't seem to mind.

"Maybe I'll go home or go work in a new village, date human men for a while. But honestly, I love the city, and I could see myself joining one of the mating houses and making great money while I help grow the pack. And then I'll raise my boys myself, making sure they're ten times better than all the wolves we've had to date."

The crazy thing is I could see her being happy doing just that.

We all hug again, and I take solace in the fact that every single word I said to her today is the truth. I don't think Justin is going to mess up, but sometimes men are idiots, and if he loses her, then she's going to move on to bigger and better things. She doesn't need a man to survive in this world. The pack has changed. There's no more need to fear the mating houses, and Faye has options now. We all do.

RYNE TAKES me to his house for dinner, and from the moment I step inside, my entire body buzzes. The aroma of an expertly prepared meal greets us, but I'm not hungry for food. I turn on him. He's so much bigger than me, but I don't care because right now I feel powerful. I push him back against the closed front door.

His eyes flare, and his large hands tighten around my waist. "What's this about?"

"I forgive you," I whisper. "And I love you. And I choose you."

The man doesn't need me to say anything more because the next second his mouth is on mine, and he's lifting me up so that my legs are wrapped tightly around him. My chest burns as passion and love swells within me, pouring out into our kiss. I grip his long hair, pulling it back from his face, and he groans into my mouth, biting at my bottom lip.

"So does this mean it's over with him?" he asks, pulling back slightly to gaze into my eyes. There's always been so much hidden in those ocean-blue depths, but now everything is right there on the surface—his want, his need, his love.

"Yes. Bell is just a friend, and he knows that now," I

whisper, my voice growing husky with need. "It's always been you, Ryne. And it will always be you."

And then we're kissing again, less desperate this time, but more untamed. He carries me upstairs to his bedroom, and we spend the rest of the night making up for lost time. Love-making is nothing new for us, but it feels like it is. It's different somehow—it's better. There's an ease to the way we touch each other, a level of trust that we never really had before. He's never going to hurt me again, and I'm never going to doubt him. We promise forever to each other with our words and our mouths and our bodies.

When I wake the next morning cocooned in his arms, I feel safer than I ever have in my life. My whole being is satiated and calm, and I'm overcome with gratitude. After everything I've been through this last year, it's a welcomed relief. Tears spring to my eyes.

"Don't cry." He shifts toward me and kisses my temple, burying his face against my hair. "Everything will be okay. We'll figure it all out. I promise."

"I'm crying because I'm so happy," I confess, and then I laugh and let the tears fall freely. "I feel like we've been given a new beginning."

He kisses each tear away and then moves to settle his body over top of mine, pinning me to the mattress in the most delicious way. "I'm the one who should be crying about new beginnings, but I have better ideas."

"Oh, and what might those ideas be?" I tease.

"I would tell you, but I think it's better if I show you."

We start to kiss again, but he pulls back before we can take things further. "I love you so much. I can't wait to marry you. Only one more week, and we'll be an engaged couple."

I smirk. "You really want to talk about marriage right now?"

"I want to do a lot of things right now, and talking about us is one of them," he confesses. "Do you want to live here after we're married, or do you want a different house?"

"I never really thought about it." And I probably should, considering it's likely I'll be getting pregnant soon. Even though we use protection, if things between us continue like they did last night, I won't be surprised if we end up having lots of babies. My mind isn't sure how ready I am to become a mother, but my heart wants to build a family with Ryne—to make his pack bigger and stronger, to give him all the things he deserves in a mate.

"Well, think about it, because it's up to you. And the wedding, what do you want to do for it? Any big plans?"

"I don't care as long as it's to you. That's all that matters."

He tsks under his breath. "I want you to have everything you could possibly want in this life, including your dream wedding, so you'd better get planning. We'll have all your favorite people there, and dancing, great food, your favorite flowers, and a huge chocolate cake because I know how much you like chocolate."

"Gotta have chocolate," I agree. "But we can decide on all that after the harvest moon. Right now, I need you to stop talking." I nip at his bruised lips to entice his mouth back down to mine. I'd like nothing more than a repeat of last night before I have to return to the manor.

"Such a bossy woman," he says between long slow kisses, but he must not mind because we don't talk again until breakfast.

I'm happier than I've ever been, but in the back of my mind, I'm terrified that something is going to come and rip that happiness away from me. The fact remains that I'm a lycan, and now that I'm the alpha to many more like me, I'm not going to be able to keep my secret hidden from the wolves for long. There are people who will kill me without hesitation if they discover the truth, and some of those people might belong to this pack, may even be living in the very same manor.

And once I'm dead, they'll come for Ryne next.

CHAPTER 30

THE DAY before the harvest moon, Ryne invites the couples over to his place to celebrate and discuss the upcoming nuptials. We have tables set up in the backyard, and the women who cook for Ryne make a beautiful charcuterie table for appetizers.

Justin and Faye show up first, followed quickly by Joanna and Grady, and then Marissa and Lev. Away from her snobby counterparts, Marissa's personality finally comes out, and she's actually really nice. I can see why Lev chose her; they make a great couple. As we mingle, I realize these will likely be the women I spend my days with. My kids will grow up with their kids.

"You get to have a wedding after all," I say, nudging Joanna.

"Yeah." She sighs wistfully, watching Grady, who is talking with Ryne and Lev across the yard. Faye and

Justin stand at one end of the table, snacking and chatting peacefully with Marissa.

"See, she had nothing to worry about," I comment.

Joanna sniffs. "Says you. Cecily was still going on this morning about how Justin was just waiting until the last minute to reveal his true choice and that he's not at all happy about Ryne inviting him here with Faye as his date."

"She's just bitter because she didn't get picked."

"Violet is too." Joanna's eyes crinkle at the sides. "That girl is the new Faye. They even look alike with the red hair."

We laugh. "True, but at least none of the girls have the threat of the mating houses anymore. They'll be fine."

"Yup, since Joy announced she's moving back to her village after the claiming, she's seemed so much happier. And I think Samantha will end up going back to her village too."

Nothing makes me happier than to know they're not going to be forced into sexual slavery, but I'm still going to miss them. Maybe I'll be able to visit, or maybe they'll come visit me in the city. Same goes for all the women currently with the panthers. I won't be surprised if several of them move home soon too.

The door opens, and I jerk my head up. All the couples are already here. Bellamy comes through the door, and my stomach drops. I haven't seen him since I told him I made my choice, and I did not expect him to choose a mate. This party is for solidified couples only.

He holds the door open, and out comes Elle. She wraps her arm around his waist and beams up at him.

I thump Joanna on the shoulder. "What the . . ."

She laughs. "Yeah. Elle made me promise not to tell you. She wanted to see your face."

I look up, and Elle meets my eyes. Then she takes Bellamy by the hand and drags him over to us. She bounces on her toes.

"Worth it," she says.

"What was?" I breathe, hardly able to believe my eyes. They look so good together, though. So happy. So *obvious.*

"Waiting until now to see your face. Seriously. That reaction was exactly what I'd hoped for."

I rub my forehead. "But when? Up until a week ago, Bell and I were talking about marriage."

"So were we. Once Ryne wanted you back, Bellamy pretty much knew he didn't have a chance. We talked about it at length several times, actually. I've pretty much been in love with him since we met."

Bellamy gazes down at her with complete adoration. "Elle was a good listener, and for the most part, we were just friends, but I'm not going to lie. I developed feelings for her some time ago. I thought it was just friendship and respect, but a few weeks ago, she kissed me. And you know, I wasn't really all that upset when you made your choice."

I reach up and give him a hug. "I'm really happy for you guys."

Then I reach for Elle. "But I don't understand why you kept pushing me toward him."

"I wanted to see you happy, and I saw how great Bell would be for someone. At that time, I didn't think he was interested in me at all." Her eyes water. "That, and I was afraid of facing my own feelings for him."

"I totally understand." And I do because I went through similar circumstances myself. She was dealing with the recent loss of her father, and a possible rejection from a man who was dating someone else must have been too painful to risk.

But I'm so glad she did risk it because look at them now.

I grin as he plants a soft kiss on her mouth. Her entire body melts, relaxing in a way I've never seen before. I have always admired Elle. From the first time I met her, I wanted to hate her for being a rival, but I simply couldn't. She's impossible not to love. She's fierce and loyal and devoted to doing the right thing—exactly like Bellamy.

They're a perfect match.

A rustling comes from behind me, and Bellamy grabs both mine and Elle's arms and jerks us back. A wolf lands right in the middle of the table, sending cheese and meat everywhere.

He scrambles up, and Ryne rushes toward him. The

wolf shifts, and I realize he's young, maybe fifteen or sixteen. His eyes widen as he takes us all in.

"I'm sorry. I didn't know you were having a party. I just saw them and thought you ought to know."

Ryne stares at the boy intently.

"Know what?" I whisper, dread building in my stomach.

The boy's lips turn into a frown, and his entire demeanor stiffens. "Anders is back, and he's brought an army with him."

No one moves for a second—it's like we can't move—until Elle grabs a towel off a chair and hands it to the boy.

"Where is he now?" Ryne asks.

"He's on his way to you. He'll be here any minute."

Ryne shakes his head in frustration. "There's no time; if there was, I'd send all the women back to Drayton Hall. But he's likely outside the front door as we speak. Men, prepare to protect your mates. I'll warn the rest of the pack, but don't engage unless it's absolutely necessary. We don't want a war breaking out if we can avoid it. Technically, he's the alpha king, so I have to obey direct orders from him, but none of you do. You only answer to me."

"We can't let him find you then," Justin says.

Ryne nods. "I think we can work around this, given a little bit of time, but Poppy's staying with me, no matter what."

I want to ask more questions, but the door flies open,

and Anders saunters out, followed by several others. He's dressed in full military regalia and even wears a damn crown on his head. I've never seen someone so blatantly boastful, but leave it to Anders to do just that.

He takes in the scene around him and smirks, and then he stalks toward Ryne. "I hear you've been making some changes around here without my permission. You've made some of your wolves very unhappy. They've come to me and begged me to fix their problem. Lucky for them, I know how to deal with you."

"You can try." Ryne glares. "But my pack is loyal *only* to me."

Anders laughs. "As of this moment, my men are taking control of the mating houses. We raided a few villages on the way to supply them with new girls. I want to make sure the Carolina Pack wolves are happy—all of them, even the ones you so foolishly kicked out."

"I gave them a choice to stay. They chose to leave. That's on them that they're no longer welcome in my pack."

"A choice? Oh, you mean taking away their rights?"

"Their right to rape women? Nobody has that right," I snap, stepping forward. "Not even you."

Anders's mouth thins as he takes me in, his nostrils flaring, before looking back to Ryne. "And tomorrow at the harvest moon, my betas will be taking the claimed girls as wives, not yours. I've brought a beta for every girl." Then Anders meets my eyes, his gaze victorious and vile. "And your dear Poppy will become my bride. That's an order, by the way, so you cannot defy it."

"Never," I say just as Ryne growls, "She's mine."

"And then, once the weddings are over," Anders speaks over us, "One of my men will become the new alpha of the Carolina Pack. I've brought dozens, and they all plan to fight. You might win the first few fights, but after that, you'll be so tired that one of them will kill you. Enjoy your last night of mortality."

He snaps his fingers, and the men he brought with him rush toward him, surrounding Anders on all sides. Protecting him. I'm not surprised; he always was afraid of Ryne.

"Stay here and guard the perimeter of this house," he instructs several of them. "No one leaves or enters. Tomorrow, you will escort them to the arena for the festival. I've got a few favorite women who have been missing me that I need to visit." Anders gives Ryne and his betas one final scathing look. "And if they're not in the mating houses, then maybe I'll have to come back here and let your whores entertain me."

Then he saunters back into the house, and everyone is so quiet we hear the front door slam.

CHAPTER 31

"HE CAN'T DO THAT." Faye is the first to speak. "Ryne's still the alpha of this pack."

But Anders is the alpha of the entire kingdom, and unless Ryne plans to separate from the other packs and face massive fallout, then Anders can dole out orders as he pleases, and Ryne will have to pass them down the chain. The Carolina Pack might be able to leave the kingdom in the future, but that's not going to help us tonight.

"Sounds like I might not be the alpha much longer," Ryne breathes out. His entire body is shaking with rage, and I'm certain he's about to take off after Anders.

Bellamy growls. "Don't let him win before you've even fought."

"It's too late," Ryne says. "I showed my hand too early."

I swallow hard because I know he's referring to all the wonderful things he did to get me back. Things he promised, things that should've been done ages ago but that he wanted to wait on. I refused to forgive him until I got my way, and now look what's happened to the pack. Maybe I should've trusted him and been patient.

Ryne was right.

But so was I.

"To hell with that." Justin steps forward. "It's not too late until we're dead, and do any of us look dead to you?"

"They're right," Grady adds, bowing to his alpha. It's the first true act of loyalty I've seen from Grady since his banishment. I shoot a glance at Joanna, who's tearing up. "You're not alone, Ryne. We're with you. You're our alpha. Nobody else. We fight with you."

Ryne looks to his betas and nods once, resolved. "Then let's go." The fur ripples over his chest, ripping his shirt clean off him.

"Don't!" I grab onto his biceps, stopping him from completing the shift. Everyone turns toward us. "Don't you see? Anders wants you to lose your temper while things are uncertain. If you guys go after him tonight while the pack is in disarray and people are scared, it'll be so much easier for him to finally kill you."

"He won't kill me," Ryne hisses. "But he can try."

"He'd have to take on all of us." Justin puffs up his chest. "We're not afraid."

"So?" I throw my hands up. Why do these men have

to be so stupid sometimes? Oh, that's right, because they're territorial wolf shifters who give into instinct before reason. "How many wolves do you think Anders brought with him tonight? Because I'm going to guess it's enough to kill you all ten times over. He has too many men, and there is no way for you to get him alone."

"What would you have us do?" Ryne cups my face in his warm hands. His voice is soft, but his eyes are frantic, and his bare chest heaves with labored breath. I hate to see him this way, but the fact that he is seriously asking for my opinion right now makes me so proud of my man. He really has changed.

But I understand why he's scared—it's not just his life on the line here. It's so many others. It's the wolves he's spent years loving. It's the humans he swore to make reparations for, to finally give them the life and the protection that was promised to them all those years ago. And it's the lycans who remained here as vulnerable humans counting on his protection.

They'll be the first to go.

"Ryne, the lycans," I whisper. "What if someone in the pack reveals them to Anders?"

There are twenty-nine who stayed after the last full moon, thirty including myself. We have too many people here who we love and didn't want to leave. The rest went back to the panther territory, Charlotte and Knox included. It's a very real possibility that the ones who stayed behind will be murdered. So many of the wolves don't want lycans here, not even after the battle at the last full moon, not even when things are mostly settled between our kinds.

I'm their alpha, which has felt like a lie considering not all of them even know who I am in my human form. I'm supposed to protect them, but I've chosen to protect myself first, and now I'm unable to help them. Luckily the wolves can't smell the lycan virus while we're human, or they'd be dead by now, and I'd have been killed months ago.

And so would've Ryne.

I stop to question that thought, because what if it's not actually true? What if his pack actually accepts him for who he is now? Like a flower rising from the frost, hope blooms within my chest. Maybe being a lycan isn't the curse I thought it was, and maybe it's not for Ryne either. This could be exactly what we need.

I take in our group one by one, grateful to be going through this with true friends—and fierce warriors. Everyone here has earned my trust. They all have so much to lose if Anders follows through on his threats at tomorrow's festival. If there's anyone who is going to help me stop that madman, it's this group. And I honestly couldn't think of anyone I'd rather follow into battle.

"Listen up. I have an idea." My voice is low as they surround me in a tight, unbreakable circle.

THE NEXT MORNING, we're taken from Ryne's house, returned to the manor to be dressed by the house mothers, and guarded by even more of Anders's men. Nobody wants to talk, and we don't act like this is the exciting affair it's supposed to be, but rather a solemn one—because we want Anders to think we're afraid. And we are afraid.

But we're also fighting for love, and love outweighs fear every single time.

If anyone should be afraid, it should be him.

We wear gorgeous dresses in an array of colors, each paired perfectly to bring out the beauty in the individual woman. Elle is a vision in daffodil yellow. Joanna is ravishing in navy blue. Faye wears emerald green like it was made for her. Marissa's skin tone glows coppery against the pastel pink. And I'm glad the dress I slide into is as red as my namesake because, tonight, I feel like shedding wolf blood and inciting a revolution.

Tonight, we fight, and we win, or we die. Either way, we'll have escaped the horror that Anders would inflict on us.

"Enough is enough," I say to these women whom I've grown to love and admire. They nod their agreement, we give each other tight hugs, and then we're ushered to the boat waiting to take us downtown.

Of course it's a boat—it's only fitting. One year ago, we were brought in a boat to this house of horror, terrified and traumatized, and then forced to compete for men and to witness our friends die or be sent away to be raped.

We've come full circle.

But if things go our way, then this will be the last time claimed women have to go through a harvest festival like this one. The time has come for it to end.

CHAPTER 32

I'VE NEVER SEEN SO MUCH red. The space around me seems to be filled with it, in every shade, in every corner, and on almost every person. It's part of the plan so we know who is on our side. The wolves wear long red scarves that will hopefully stay on when they shift. We tested it a bit last night, and it seemed to work, so Ryne put out the call for his pack to wear a scarf to tonight's festival if they were with him.

It's the one thing we were certain Anders would notice. And I hope it intimidates him. He brought his angry army, but there are more of us than there are of his people. By a lot.

And we're just as angry as they are—maybe even more so.

The sun hangs low in the sky, painting it in vibrant brushstrokes of orange. The Harvest Moon Festival always starts at sunset, and we'll have about twenty minutes before the moon rises enough to trigger the renewals. Once that happens, the fight begins.

Elle grips my hand. "Are you ready?"

"Yes. You?"

She smooths her dress and looks across the stage. The new claimed girls Anders brought in last night are with us, as are Samantha, Violet, and Cecily. Madame Delphine and a few others will get them to a safe house once the fighting begins, but they don't know that. They don't know anything of what's to come. There are twice as many claimed women as last year, so many whom I've never even met before, and very few are meant to get husbands today. Anders only brought them here to feed them to the mating houses tonight. Because despite so many girls being here in pretty dresses, the number of betas taking wives is the same. Instead of Ryne, Justin, Grady, Bellamy, and Lev standing on the edge of the stage in suits and ties, it's Anders and four of his cronies. They leer at us, and it doesn't take much to imagine what they might be thinking.

"We're doing this for them," Elle reminds me, looking toward the frightened women surrounding us. Samantha catches my eye and frowns. Her face is tight with worry, and I know she regrets staying here when she had the opportunity to go to The Sanctuary more than once—but now it's too late.

"We're doing this for all of us," I say.

And then I look back behind the stage to where the new claimed girls are standing, twenty innocent young women forcefully gathered from the villages by Anders's men. That was me last year, but so much has happened in a year that it feels like a lifetime ago. I recognize the girl I met, Laura, among them. She nods to me, a solemn expression on her face. I return the hello and quickly turn away. She didn't know what to expect when I had first met her, but she sure does now. They all do—the secrets are out, and everyone is horrified. These girls are only here to be turned into baby makers and wives and whores.

Not if I can help it.

Joanna steps between us and wiggles her eyebrows at Elle. "Have fun with Bellamy last night?"

Elle flushes. "How can you talk about things like that right now?"

Joanna bounces back and forth on her feet and rubs the back of her neck. "The tension is too much. Gotta do something, right? I know I had fun last night. I hope you two did as well."

"We were too busy preparing for today." I sigh. "I didn't even sleep."

Joanna giggles. "Neither did I. And neither did Elle, based on that blush."

Faye puts her arm around Elle. "It's okay. You can talk about it. Justin and I . . ."

"It's time." Madame Delphine interrupts us. "Come up front, Poppy."

I gather my skirts and make my way to the front of the group to stand next to Samantha and Joy, careful not to twist my ankles in these shoes. They'll be destroyed when I shift into my lycan form, which I'm not sad about. But the dress. The dress, I love. Joanna promised to make me another once this is all over. I squeeze both Samantha's and Joy's hands, and they give me terrified expressions. I wish I could tell them I have a plan to save them from the mating houses, but I can't risk it, so I just squeeze their hands again and hope they'll stay out of the way when the time comes.

Ryne stands at the front of the stage, and Anders joins him, his bodyguard betas right there with him every step of the way. Ryne tries to speak, but Anders cuts him off then starts droning on about the changes Ryne made, how he's going to put things back to the way they were, and how Ryne is a disgraced alpha. I have to resist rolling my eyes.

"And so, as alpha king, it is my privilege to choose a bride from among your women, and I've always been partial to Poppy. And my men, well, they want brides, and I don't think anyone who has remained loyal to Ryne in his madness deserves them." The new betas descend on us, grabbing us roughly by the arms and dragging us to the front of the stage. We don't fight it. Not yet anyway.

The beta who has my arm shoves me next to Anders, who puts his sleazy arm around me. I hold my tongue. I have to be docile for just a few more minutes. Ryne is only a few paces away, and he glowers at us like he wants to rip Anders's head off. Anders squeezes me tighter into his body, taunting Ryne. But Ryne doesn't take the bait.

He turns back to the crowd. "You all know my stance on this. I will not go quietly. Poppy is my fated mate; I will not let Anders take her. There will be a fight, and you will have a new alpha king by morning."

Anders pulls me in even tighter, crushing my body against his. My left shoulder screams in protest, but still, I don't move. Ryne continues, "But first, you know the marriage bond is the strongest thing we have. Once a woman is married, she's not allowed to be with another wolf. Anders, you support the old ways, so you respect that tradition, yes?"

Anders rolls his eyes. "Of course I do. Which is why, once I marry Poppy, you can't have her."

"Okay, then." Ryne steps toward us. Justin, Bellamy, Lev, and Grady jump up onto the stage to back Ryne. They're all dressed in suits, and I must say they look far more handsome than Anders's crew. "See, last night, you made it so we couldn't leave my home, so we had a little fun of our own."

Anders scoffs, and his hands begin to roam my body. "I think you've had enough fun with this one, Ryne. It's about time I show her how a real man should be entertained."

He pinches my backside, and I squirm, heat rushing through me. It takes everything I have not to punch him right here and throw him off me. My mind fills with images of the first time I saw him do this to someone—to

Willow—and how I was forced to do nothing. I'm not going to sit around this time. Only a few more minutes . . .

Ryne steps toward us, his voice going dangerously low. "Get your hands off my wife."

Anders stills. "Wife? What are you talking about?"

"We married our women last night, so you can't have them."

A hush falls over the crowd, and Anders goes unsteady on his feet. He's been bested. There's nothing he can do to claim me now, and he knows it. I grin, wanting to fall right back into Ryne's arms, but I don't. Not yet. I do lock eyes with him, though, and he grins right back at me.

After explaining the plan last night, Ryne married the others, and Grady married us. The ceremonies were beautiful and simple. All that was needed was the alpha's blessing and a special exchange of vows with a kiss. None of us wore fancy dresses. There wasn't chocolate cake or bouquets of flowers. We didn't even dance, but the kiss Ryne gave me was sweeter than any before. It was a promise of forever even if forever was only a day, and a promise I'll never forget.

Anders shoves me to the floor. I play along, falling to my knees. Soon after, my girlfriends are all shoved down as well. Our men are with us instantly, lifting us to our feet. Ryne wraps me in his embrace, shielding me with his body.

"All you accomplished was making sure that these

women will be widows." Anders sneers at Ryne. "Because it won't be long until you're no longer the alpha of the Carolina Pack, and once you're gone, your traitors will be disposed of. No more banishment. I'll kill them myself if I have to."

Several wolves cheer, and others growl as the tension grows. There are two opposing sides, and we're at the breaking point. Only one can win this.

My bones creak, and I panic for a second. The moon is rising faster than we thought. But this could be a good thing, it could mean that none of Ryne's pack has turned on my lycans. There's no way Anders knows we're even here and about to attack his men because, even now, I can spot several of my people scattered among the crowd. This also means that Ryne's pack is loyal because, last night when he used his telepathic link to command them not to reveal the lycans' identities, they followed his orders. They want Anders dead. They want the new way of life Ryne has offered them. And they know the lycans can help them get it.

Change is in the air.

I widen my eyes at Ryne. He nods to show he's gotten the message, and then, without warning, my body expands, and my dress rips to shreds.

Anders staggers backward and gapes at me. "What? How?"

Down among the wolves, the bloodbath begins.

My lycans have returned, this time prepared to fight

for freedom from the tyranny of Anders and his wolves. After tonight, nothing will be the same.

Ryne shifts into his wolf form and pounces on Anders before Anders can shift. The alpha king lands flat on his back and quickly shifts into his wolf, pushing Ryne away and scrambling to his haunches. I back up to see that Madame Delphine and the claimed girls are already gone. Ryne's betas and all the lunas stand behind him, an arsenal of snarling wolves.

Anders stares at all of them for a second.

And then the coward turns and flings himself off the stage, running from the fight.

CHAPTER 33

KILL HIM, Ryne says to me as we make chase, but those two words come as a shock.

But you need to do it so you're the next alpha king, I argue. *That's the plan.*

Anders is fast, running through the streets at full speed, darting between buildings, his brown coat gleaming under the moonlight before falling back into the shadows. But we're faster.

Do you want to be the wife of the alpha king? Ryne challenges. *Do you want to move to Chicago where we'll always be looking over our shoulders? Have wolves constantly arguing that a lycan isn't fit to be queen or that a hybrid can't be king? Because I don't want that life for you, Poppy. And I've already made up my mind to tell my pack the truth about my lycan once this is over.*

Well, when he puts it that way, I guess he's right, but

I'd do all those things and more for the people I love. If it means protecting the humans and getting to be with Ryne, then I'm happy to be the next queen, even a queen that half the kingdom would want dead. Whatever it takes.

I have an idea that will put someone else in the position of alpha king, someone who will be much better at it than I ever could be, but first, we need Anders dead.

Anders being dead is all I can think about at this point. I remember all the times he groped me, all the lewd comments he made, the way his eyes would linger on me just to make me uncomfortable, the countless women he raped over the years, the poor wives he's buried too young. I think about sweet innocent Nova and her cold body floating lifelessly in the river, a woman who was fated to his son, a son he should've loved. I think of Lexi and the way he brutalized her in her own bedroom while she slept, then how he turned on Joanna and Grady and even Ryne.

And then I think of my Willow—and that's all I need.

Fueled by rage, I leap harder and faster than I ever have, landing on Anders's back. He snarls, but I don't even stop to think about it. I attack, clamping down on his neck with my razor-sharp teeth, and I throw myself back so that his wolf body twists. He howls, and I do it again, grabbing onto his hind legs this time to twist him into an odd angle. His neck snaps, but I don't stop until his head is clean off his body. I toss it to the ground, an arc of blood spraying across the alleyway. And then I drop his body.

Finally.

Ryne and I stand there, breathing deeply for a long minute, staring at the decapitated body. It's only fair that Anders went this way—though, he deserved far worse.

You know what? I tell Ryne. *I actually feel a lot better.*

He chuckles, and then side by side, we race back to the battleground.

It's a total mess. There are more casualties on both sides than we expected. Everyone must have felt the alpha king die, but since a wolf didn't kill him, they're not bowing down to Ryne. I should've thought this through before I took him up on his offer. It's the same issue we had when I killed his father. Now there will be battles for a new alpha king—and the cycle will just continue on and on.

I was a fool, letting revenge get the better of me, and Ryne was thinking of our relationship before the betterment of the pack. We made a mistake.

"Oh, no you don't!"

I hear a familiar voice in the fight—Faye's voice. She's not supposed to be here. All the human women were supposed to get to safety with Madame Delphine. But sure enough, I follow the sound of her shrill yelling to find her fighting off an angry wolf. She's got two long swords in her hands, each already dripping with blood. I'm not sure where she got them, but she handles them expertly, slicing them toward her opponent.

Joanna is at her side.

And with them are Grady, with his three legs, and Justin—both in their wolf forms.

The group of wolves they are fighting are bigger and angrier than most of the others, fueled by the death of their alpha, or perhaps they were some who belonged to this pack before Ryne kicked them out, and now they're back for revenge. But it doesn't matter. Whoever they are, they're out for blood—so they must be stopped.

I sprint toward them, prepared to defend my friends, when one of them breaks past Faye's swords and catches her belly with his nasty teeth. He slices her abdomen to ribbons, and she slumps over, blood pooling before falling flat on her back, dropping the swords altogether.

No. This can't be happening.

I leap forward, ready to help. I'll bite her if I have to. She can become a lycan and might even like it, but she can't die. She can't.

Justin beats me to her. He throws the wolf from his wife and howls, nudging her with his muzzle. But she doesn't move. Her eyes stare up into nothingness, glossy and unblinking. The Faye we all know, the Faye I learned to love like a sister, is gone.

His cry shatters my heart, and then he's turning on her murderer. But he's distracted and doesn't see the second wolf that pounces from behind. In all of two seconds, Justin's neck is sliced open, and he's bleeding out too. In his final moments, he shifts back into his human form and crawls to Faye, resting his bloodied body against her, adding more red to her already-stained emerald gown. Suddenly, I hate red more than anything because he's gone too.

I can't believe it.

No.

"Justin was my cousin, you bastard!" Joanna screams, dashing toward the wolves. While it's true that he was her cousin, Joanna barely got to spend time with him, and now he's gone forever. I'm right there with her, and so are Grady and Ryne. We make quick work of the remaining wolves, adding them to the list of casualties, but this time, I don't feel any better. I just feel empty.

We look around us, and all we see is loss. The battle continues to rage all around, and there are still several hours before the sun rises. Many more will be killed before the night is over. How many more of us have to die? When will it be enough? Ryne leaves my side, and I follow, not daring to let him out of my sight.

He leaps for the empty stage, and I stay back. He needs to do this part alone.

WOLVES. LYCANS. STOP. His voice hits my mind with so much power that there is no question. It reverberates through my brain. Most of the fighting stops, but some still continues. He repeats his words three more times, each time more powerful than the last. My head aches with the pressure.

Until it's done. Nobody moves. All the fighting has stopped, and everyone—wolves and lycans—gathers near the stage. It's strange seeing them all intermingled together, blood matted in fur and dropping from wounds. We're all so different, but our blood is the same.

We have fought valiantly tonight for the things we believe in. We fight against each other, and we barely even know what we're fighting for. It's time for a change. Many of you have recognized that, and some of you wish to cling to traditions and things of the past. But nothing ever stays the same. Once again, we have lost our alpha king without a new one being chosen, and he won't be chosen tonight.

Tonight, we rest. Go home and sleep. Mourn your losses. Tomorrow morning, we will meet at the arena. All are welcome—lycan, wolves, and humans—and together, we'll find a way to coexist, or I will die fighting for it. I don't know about you, but I cannot bear the loss of another friend.

His shoulders fall a little, and then he jumps from the stage. I worry that someone will attack him, especially since he just spoke to wolves *and* lycans, but nobody does. The crowd parts to let him trudge toward me. Together, lycan and wolf, we head toward his home. A few bow, publicly declaring their allegiance, and I wonder at his words earlier.

He may not want to be alpha king, but his pack wants him to be. Despite everything, they believe he's the best leader for the job, and they're right.

I'm not sure I'm willing to let him sacrifice that for me.

CHAPTER 34

THE PLAN IS to start the meeting at nine. At eight-thirty, all of Ryne's betas, Madame Delphine, and everyone from Drayton Hall meet outside Ryne's house. My house now too, I guess. It's strange to think of it that way. I never really pictured myself somewhere so grand, but wherever my husband goes, I go.

We pile into several cars and slowly make our way over to the arena. Ryne and I are alone in his car. Callum was going to drive us, but he's still tending to the wounded and hasn't come back yet. Neither one of us has really spoken this morning, both lost in our own thoughts.

"Your betas know," I say.

"Know what?"

"That I'm a lycan and that you are too. And they still follow you."

"How can they know?"

"Everyone saw me change last night, and you were able to speak to them all. They know."

Ryne flexes his fingers around the steering wheel. "That makes today all the more dangerous. They could kill you. And me."

"But they won't. They would've last night. Ryne. I don't know what you have planned for this morning, but I think you should fight for alpha king. You are the only one who can make the changes stick. They'll follow you. All of them."

Ryne shakes his head. "No. I won't do it. You deserve a better life than that after all that you've been through. I'll keep my little pack here if they'll have me, but I'm not fighting for alpha king."

"Ryne. This is stupid. If you don't fight for it and win, then we could end up exactly where we were before. I've been through enough that I can handle that life."

He shakes his head. "No. Poppy, I'm not doing it."

"You're not your father, Ryne. Things will be different if it's you."

He pulls to the side of the road and parks then takes my hand, threading our fingers together. "That kind of power corrupts. I can't risk going back to who I was, and I can't risk putting a target on your back either."

"But it will be different this time—"

"Look at me," he grinds out, and I do, taking in his beaten-down expression and wanting nothing more than to see him smile again. He squeezes my hand. "I allowed horrible things to happen within my pack for years because I was afraid to challenge my father. I know I'm not him, but I'll never put myself into a position to become like him again. Ultimately, I'm responsible for what happened here since the day I became alpha, and I need to take accountability."

I shake my head. He's not getting it.

"All I want is you, Poppy. And us. I love my pack, and I love being an alpha, but I love you the most. You're my life now. My family. My wife."

My eyes water. I never asked for any of this, and I'll always mourn what could have been if Willow had lived, but getting to be loved by Ryne is the best thing that ever happened to me. "I love you too," I whisper.

A hot tear releases, and he kisses it away. "Trust me," he whispers. "I'm going to make things as right as I can, and that means I can't be the next alpha king. I have too much blood on my hands."

I hate that he blames himself for so much, but it doesn't make it untrue. Maybe he'll never forgive himself, maybe the humans he hurt will never forgive him, but I do.

"Okay, I trust you." I kiss him softly and release a long sigh. "Let's go."

As we near the arena, we see people everywhere crowding around it. When Ryne steps out of the car, a hush falls over the crowd. We make our way through the group. In the daylight it's impossible to tell who's shifter, lycan, or human. But I think they are all mixed together.

The arena is completely full, and after we make our way to the podium, we see more and more people piling in. They squeeze together, fill the stairs, and crowd along the top. How many of these were Anders's men? Are they all even from the Carolina Pack? I've never seen it like this before, and it makes me uneasy. This could be it. This could be where we all die.

Grady and Joanna appear at our side. "These aren't just wolves from Carolina," Grady confirms. "Word got out. Neighboring packs are here too."

That turns the trickle of fear within me into an all-out downpour, but I force myself to push it aside. I have to be strong; too many people are counting on me.

Ryne waits until it's not possible for another person to get through the door, and then he steps up to the stage on the arena field, pulling me up with him.

"I've never been comfortable with the mating houses and our lifestyle." His strong voice echoes over the microphone as everyone quiets. "But given who my father was, I felt powerless to make any changes. Plus, I knew once I tried, I'd be killed for it. And so I was a coward, and I bear responsibility for so much pain." He trails off, and people exchange nervous glances. "But at the last claiming, something incredible happened. I found my fated mate."

He smiles at me, and I have to resist rolling my eyes. He's going to use me as an excuse not to take the mantle he was meant for. But I smile back.

"And she showed me that there are some things

worth fighting for. We've had some bumps along the way. She was bitten by a lycan, and then in the middle of the fight to take out my father, she accidentally bit me."

Every single person in the room hangs on his words. I hadn't realized that he was going to lay our secrets bare to be judged, and it terrifies me.

"Lycans have far more control over themselves than us wolves give them credit for. In fact, it's only the first shift that they are bloodthirsty. I've recently learned that most of the attacks during the full moons were to rescue the women we'd enslaved, not kill them. Because of the bite Poppy gave me, I have lycan blood running through my veins, and it did not kill me. I suspect that is because of the bond Poppy and I share as mates.

"We need change. We need peace, and we need freedom for all—shifters, lycans, and humans. And for ourselves, we need to stop fighting to the death. We're losing too many good wolves that way."

A cheer goes up in the crowd, and I realize that many of the wolves feel the same way. Maybe no fight will be necessary today.

"That is why I will not fight for alpha king."

No one says anything for a moment, and then a few people begin to chant. "Ryne. Ryne. Ryne."

And it grows until it fills the whole stadium.

I nudge him and lean up to speak into his ear. "No fight will be necessary. But you will be alpha king if they have any say in it."

He shakes his head, and we wait for the chanting to

die off. “You would have a king with no fight?” he asks into the microphone, and a roar fills our ears.

“You would have me be your king?”

Again, a cheer goes up.

He swivels around and searches the small group that came with us today. He jumps off the podium, makes his way to Elle, and drags her back up here with us. Her eyes are wide, and her lips are pulled into a tight smile. She clearly doesn’t know what he’s doing, but I think I do, and pride wells in my chest.

“What are you doing?” she hisses, but he doesn’t say anything at all. He just grins.

“I meant it when I said we need change. Most of you know the luna, Elle Montgomery. She’s been a driving force for change and a key leader of the Resistance. Would you have a queen instead of a king?”

Elle’s face pales, but she doesn’t falter. There is a cheer again, but this time it’s distinctly female, and murmurs have broken out among the crowd.

“I think you overestimated their ability to accept change,” Elle whispers. But Ryne shakes his head.

“Just wait a moment for them to think through this.”

A chant begins again, but this time, it’s not Ryne’s name. It’s Elle’s.

“Elle. Elle. Elle.”

And just like that.

Without another death.

Ryne waves his hand toward Elle. “Get ready,

because now we march to Chicago together to put Elle on the throne."

She's stunned, but she nods, and then the crowd erupts into a frenzy. There's no stopping us—there's no stopping Elle.

We will have an alpha queen.

EPILOGUE

FIVE YEARS LATER

THE HARVEST FESTIVAL IS TONIGHT, and I can't wait. More matches were made this year than any previous, and so many of the girls are head over heels in love with their wolves. We're sure to have an incredible wedding season soon, which is always fun for the pack.

There were also an unusual number of fated mate pairs that popped up this year. It reminded me of my claimed year, though I try not to think about that if I can help it. I used to have nightmares about the horrors I went through, but time has soothed those into unhappy memories better left to the past. And every year since we put Elle on the throne has been better than the last.

"There you are." Abi plops down onto the blanket beside me, reaching for my picnic basket. "I'm famished. What did you bring?"

"Practically my whole garden." I laugh. "I had to harvest the last of it this week."

"Mama, I'm not hungry," her son Orien complains with a pout, his huge chocolate brown eyes blinking at his mother. "Can I go play with Faye and Willow?" He looks around, confused. "Where are they?"

My twin daughters are currently hiding among the array of autumn leaves, but even from here, I can hear their sweet voices giggling. Just like me and my sister, they love to climb trees, and even at three years old, they're already experts. I attribute their natural athleticism to Ryne's alpha genes, but their taste for adventure is mine.

I point to a nearby tree. "They're up there."

Abi rolls her eyes and pats her son on the head. "Fine, go play, but you're not getting dessert until you eat something healthy." He's gone before she can even finish her sentence.

We laugh and get to work on setting up the picnic, and soon the others are joining us, blankets spread throughout the lawn in a patchwork of friendship. It's something we claimed women do often but especially on the days of the festivals. So many of us are haunted by the memories of the things that happened during those dark times, and we don't want anyone to be alone on days like today.

The park fills with mothers and their children—some are the beta wives, but many are not. The children play, and we women chat among ourselves, happy to enjoy the crisp autumn under these circumstances. The shifter men aren't invited to these quarterly picnics. These are just for us.

"Hi, Jasmine," Abi says to a woman setting up her picnic near us. "It's great to see you. How are your sons?"

The woman is about fifteen years older than us and endured so much more than we ever had to. Abi once told me that Jasmine was one of the only friends she made during her time in the mating house. Nobody thought Jasmine would ever see her children again, but Jasmine always believed. Luckily, the pack kept records of which women had which children, and Jasmine was reunited with all eleven of hers.

Eleven.

Just the thought of bearing that many children makes my body ache.

"They're doing great. Only my youngest four could come out today, though. The others are too old for games." She rolls her eyes, and we chat merrily as she finishes setting up her picnic. Then she's running off to play with her kids, her own childlike nature having never left her, despite everything.

"Eleven kids," Abi whispers. "And most of them were teenagers before she ever got to see them again."

I take her hand and squeeze because we're thinking the same thing. That could have been us.

"Anything new with you two?" Joanna asks as she sits down between me and Abi. She waggles her eyes at our friend. "Any new romantic prospects?"

It's a nice distraction. Joanna always did have the best timing.

Abi shrugs and shakes her head. After her son was born, she vowed never to touch another man again. So far, she's kept that promise. "I'm happier staying single. Orien is enough for me, anyway. He's my world."

Joanna and I nod because we understand in our own ways. Grady is Joanna's world, and when she told him she didn't want to have children, he was fine with that. All he wanted was whatever made her happiest. She practically runs that textile village now, but she always makes a point to come to the city for the festival picnics.

And as for me, Ryne and the twins are my world—as is the child currently growing in my womb, a child who is sure to be another girl.

That was the surprise of a lifetime. Soon after things settled down and people started coupling, we discovered that shifter men and lycan women nearly always have female shifter offspring.

That changed everything.

The mating houses still exist, but they're voluntary and are starting to die out. The claiming, however, has grown exponentially. So much so that three more manors have had to be opened to accommodate everyone just in the Carolina Pack. Many human women and female lycans elect to spend a year dating wolf men. Some are betas, but lower ranks are also invited to come date women. Marriages are encouraged but not required. Anyone can walk away at any time. If a couple does get engaged under Ryne's blessing, then they can live together in the city, usually raising a family together. Or they can go live among the villages with the humans.

My own parents stayed in our village, but Evan says he's going to become a lycan when he grows up, just like his sister. It scares me to think about that, but it's also not my place to stop him. Same as it's not my place to stop so many humans from taking on the lycan virus, despite the risks. Turns out lycans also age slower than humans, and a lot of people want that opportunity. What worries me most about Evan is that he'll leave us for another pack or to live among the panthers like so many others did. Charlotte and Knox moved south, and we've only heard from them twice in the years since. They wanted to start over, and I can't say I blame them, but that doesn't mean I don't miss them from time to time.

Our pack has thrived, and so have all the others, as far as I know. In the five years since Elle enforced the changes Ryne started, the kingdom has exploded with new babies—male and female wolf shifters and more lunas than ever. Of course there were dissenters, but they left for the wilds or got in line, and no more abuse is tolerated in any of the packs. Elle and Bellamy are the best thing that ever could've happened to the kingdom, and I wonder how many little luna girls want to grow up to be just like their fearless queen. My daughters certainly do.

But I don't . . .

Ryne was right not to put us on that throne. We're so

happy where we're at, living in a restored farmhouse on the edge of town. I spend my days tending our gardens and raising our children while he takes care of the pack. Only on full-moon nights does adventure still call to me, and that's when I roam the forest with my own pack—a pack that I turned the title of alpha over to Callum years ago. Otherwise, it's a quiet life for me, filled with love and family and friends. It's all I ever wanted.

I lie back, hands on my large belly, listening to my friends chat merrily as they devour the food from my garden. The blue sky seems to stretch on forever, a reminder of the bluest eyes I've ever seen and the man that fate chose for me. But I know that even if fate hadn't intervened, I still would've chosen him, and he would've chosen me. And that's a choice nobody can take from us. Not ever.

The End

DEAR READER

What a wild ride, huh? We're so pleased with the way Poppy's story concluded—these characters sure made it interesting! Thank you for reading the series and we hope you'll continue to enjoy our books. If you haven't already, please write us a written review on Amazon and Goodreads. As indie authors, reviews make a big difference and mean a lot. By the way, if you haven't read The Alpha's Kiss bonus scene yet, access is available by going to both of our Facebook reader groups:

FB.com/groups/ninasreadingparty

FB.com/groups/kimberlylothreleaseparty

We love you guys! Thank you for going on this journey with us.

Yours,

Nina & Kimberly

ALSO BY NINA WALKER

YA dystopian Fantasy

The Color Alchemist Series

NA Paranormal & Romantic Fantasy

The Dragon Blessed Series

Urban Fantasy

The Vampires & Vices Series

YA Dystopian fantasy standalone

Dark ocean princess

Adult Romantic Comedy by Grace Costello

Twinfluence

Ivy League Liars

ALSO BY KIMBERLY LOTH

YA Paranormal Romance & Fantasy

The Dragon Kings

The Dragon King Chronicles

Circus of the Dead

Circus of the Dead Chronicles

The Thorn Chronicles

Stella and Sol

Sons of the Sand

YA Contemporary fiction

Bittersweet

Something About Forever

Sweet Romance by Kimmy Loth

Michigan Millionaires

ACKNOWLEDGMENTS

Thank you to all the readers who championed this series. We love you! And thank you to our cover designer MiblArt, editors Ailene Kubricky and Cookie Lynn Publishing, our proof readers, arc readers, and so many others. Special thanks to Virginia Wall and Phi Pilgrim, and to our amazing friends and family. We couldn't have done this without your continued support.

You're the best!

ABOUT THE AUTHORS

Nina Walker is a USA Today and Amazon Top 100 Bestselling author. Living near the beautiful red mountains of Southern Utah, she writes across multiple fantasy genres and co-writes under the romantic comedy pen name, Grace Costello.

Kimberly Loth has lived all over the world. From the isolated woods of the Ozarks to exotic city of Cairo. Currently she resides in the Missouri Ozarks with her husband and their spunky dog, Maisy. She's the author of the Amazon bestselling series The Dragon Kings. In her free time she volunteers at church, reads, and travels as often as possible.

www.ingramcontent.com/pod-product-compliance
Lightning Source LLC
Chambersburg PA
CBHW020336310726
48979CB00015B/2385/J

* 9 7 8 1 9 5 0 0 9 3 4 2 7 *